For *centuries* [illegible] posses[illegible] e omnisc[illegible] o create a[illegible]

But this [illegible] locked in [illegible] *ntasy.*

Until sudd[illegible] *[illegible]cably,* two members [illegible] aptain Kirk's crew are singled out and are mysteriously endowed with *super-human powers* . . . They are capable of doing *anything* they want. They can create and they can destroy.

And when this incredible power is directed against Captain Kirk, he is forced to enter a world . . .

WHERE NO MAN HAS GONE BEFORE

ANOTHER **FOTONOVEL** TM
YOU WILL ENJOY—

THE CITY ON THE EDGE OF FOREVER

STAR TREK™*

WHERE NO MAN HAS GONE BEFORE

written by **SAMUEL A. PEEPLES**

adapted from the television series
created by **GENE RODDENBERRY**

BANTAM BOOKS · TORONTO · NEW YORK · LONDON

RLI: VLM 6 (VLR 5–7) / IL 5+

WHERE NO MAN HAS GONE BEFORE
A Bantam Book / November 1977

ISBN 0-553-12726-8

Published simultaneously in the United States and Canada

Bantam Books are published by Bantam Books, Inc. Its trademark, consisting of the words "Bantam Books" and the portrayal of a bantam, is registered in the United States Patent Office and in other countries. Marca Registrada. Bantam Books, Inc., 666 Fifth Avenue, New York, New York 10019.

PRINTED IN THE UNITED STATES OF AMERICA

0 9 8 7 6 5 4 3 2

As a writer and avid Star Trek fan, it was with great trepidation that I opened the cover of your first Star Trek Fotonovel. Would this be just another cheap rip-off? What would you do to ruin the memory of my favorite characters? Why didn't everyone just leave what was a great T.V. show alone?

You can imagine my surprise when what I saw was a beautifully rendered, tastefully written book about the real adventures of the Starship *Enterprise* — as good as, and in some ways even better than, the television series that we all love. As good as the series because it was the original story, not just some hokey concoction by people who never even saw the set, let alone wrote the show. Better because it lasted. No longer was I subject to the whims of some anonymous network programmer. I could take a trip aboard the *Enterprise* whenever and wherever I felt like it. If I liked a remark that Spock made to Kirk, well, then I could read it again and again.

Not only that, but your Fotonovel stood on its own as a beautiful book, worthy to be put out for guests to peek at.

And here is your second book. Congratulations! If possible it's even better than your first.

But watch out. There are millions of Trekkies like me who are keeping their eye on you. And if you let us down, we'll be forced to apply the Vulcan nerve pinch!

Shelley Katz

Shelley Katz, a California based writer whose past works include the novel Alligator, *is currently working on a major screenplay for Paramount Pictures.*

CAST LIST

James R. Kirk, Captain

William Shatner

A man in his mid-30's, whose strong independent nature and sympathetic soul make him a natural leader whose overriding concern is always the safety and well being of his ship and its crew.

Mr. Spock, First Officer

Leonard Nimoy

Chief science officer, of Vulcan and Terran heritage, which accounts for his highly analytical mind and extraordinary strength. His life is almost totally ruled by reason and logic.

Lt. Cmdr. Gary Mitchell, Second Officer

Gary Lockwood

Chief Navigator. A former student of Kirk's at the Star Fleet Academy and a personal friend who has an unbridled interest in women.

Elizabeth Dehner, M.D.

Sally Kellerman

Psychiatrist assigned to the *Enterprise* to study crew reactions under stress situations. Her cold professional manner masks a warm and compassionate heart.

Montgomery Scott, Lt. Commander

James Doohan

Chief Engineer. A middle-aged man of Scottish ancestry whose knowledge of the ship's engineering equipment is unchallenged.

Sulu, Chief Helmsman

George Takei

An Oriental man of unquestioned competence.

Lee Kelso, Lieutenant

Paul Carr

Helmsman.

Mark Piper, M.D. Senior Surgeon

Paul Fix

Head of Life Sciences Department.

Yeoman Smith

Andrea Dromm

Lt. Alden, Communications Officer

Lloyd Haynes

Guard

Eddie Paskey

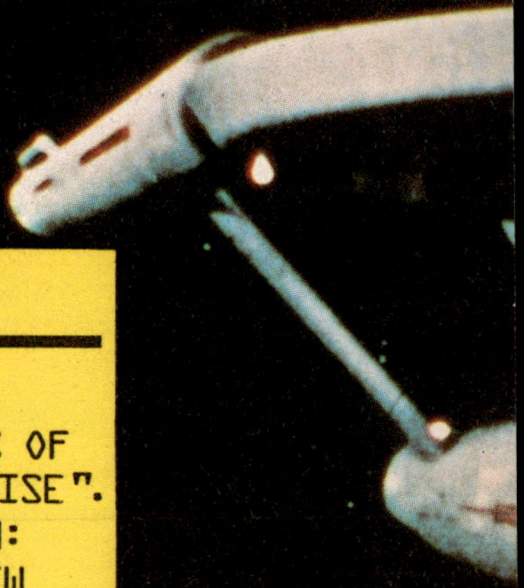

SPACE:

THE FINAL FRONTIER

THESE ARE THE VOYAGES OF THE STARSHIP "ENTERPRISE". ITS FIVE YEAR MISSION: TO EXPLORE STRANGE NEW WORLDS...TO SEEK OUT NEW LIFE AND NEW CIVILIZATIONS...TO BOLDLY GO...

WHERE NO MAN HAS GONE BEFORE

CAPTAIN'S LOG:

STARDATE 1312.4

THE IMPOSSIBLE HAS HAPPENED. FROM DIRECTLY AHEAD, WE'RE PICKING UP A RECORDED DISTRESS SIGNAL USING THE CALL LETTERS OF A VESSEL WHICH HAS BEEN MISSING FOR OVER TWO CENTURIES. DID ANOTHER EARTHSHIP ONCE PROBE OUT OF THE GALAXY AS WE INTEND TO DO? WHAT HAPPENED TO IT OUT THERE? IS THIS SOME WARNING THEY'VE LEFT BEHIND?

A friendly game of chess is in progress between Captain Kirk and his First Officer, Mr. Spock. But Kirk's attention keeps wandering. He can't take his eyes off the viewscreen.
Your move, Captain.

But the strange signals the Starship has been picking up continue to puzzle Kirk.
Why the **delay?** We should have intercepted by **now.** The bridge **said** they'd call . . . .
Captain, I must **warn** you. I'll have you **checkmated** your next move.

Spock's seriousness, even in leisure moments, never fails to amuse Kirk.
Have I mentioned that you play a very **irritating** game of chess, Mr. Spock?
Irritating? Ah, yes . . . one of your **Earth** emotions.
We shall **see** just how well the Captain deals with irritation as soon as I take my **next turn.**
But there **is** no next turn. For Kirk's move places Spock's king in a checkmated position from which there is **no possible escape!**

Having studied the board and realizing that the game is lost . . .
Certain you don't know what irritation is???
It **is** possible, considering that one of my ancestors married a **human female!**
Terrible, having **bad blood** like that!

Bridge to Briefing Lounge.
Go ahead, Mr. Kelso. We have you on the viewscreen.
Object is now within tractor beam range, but its size is too small for visual contact. The vessel only reads about one meter in diameter.
That's not large enough even for a lifeboat.
Mr. Kelso, can we bring it aboard?
We can, sir, if you want to risk it.

Lock onto it, Mr. Kelso.
I **sincerely hope** the Captain knows what he's **doing!**
*This is what Kirk has been waiting for! **At last** they will be able to find out what happened to that old spaceship. Hurriedly they rush to the Transporter Room where Mr. Scott, the ship's Chief Engineer, is plotting the coordinates needed to pinpoint the **exact location** of the mysterious object.*
Can you get a **fix** on it, Scotty?

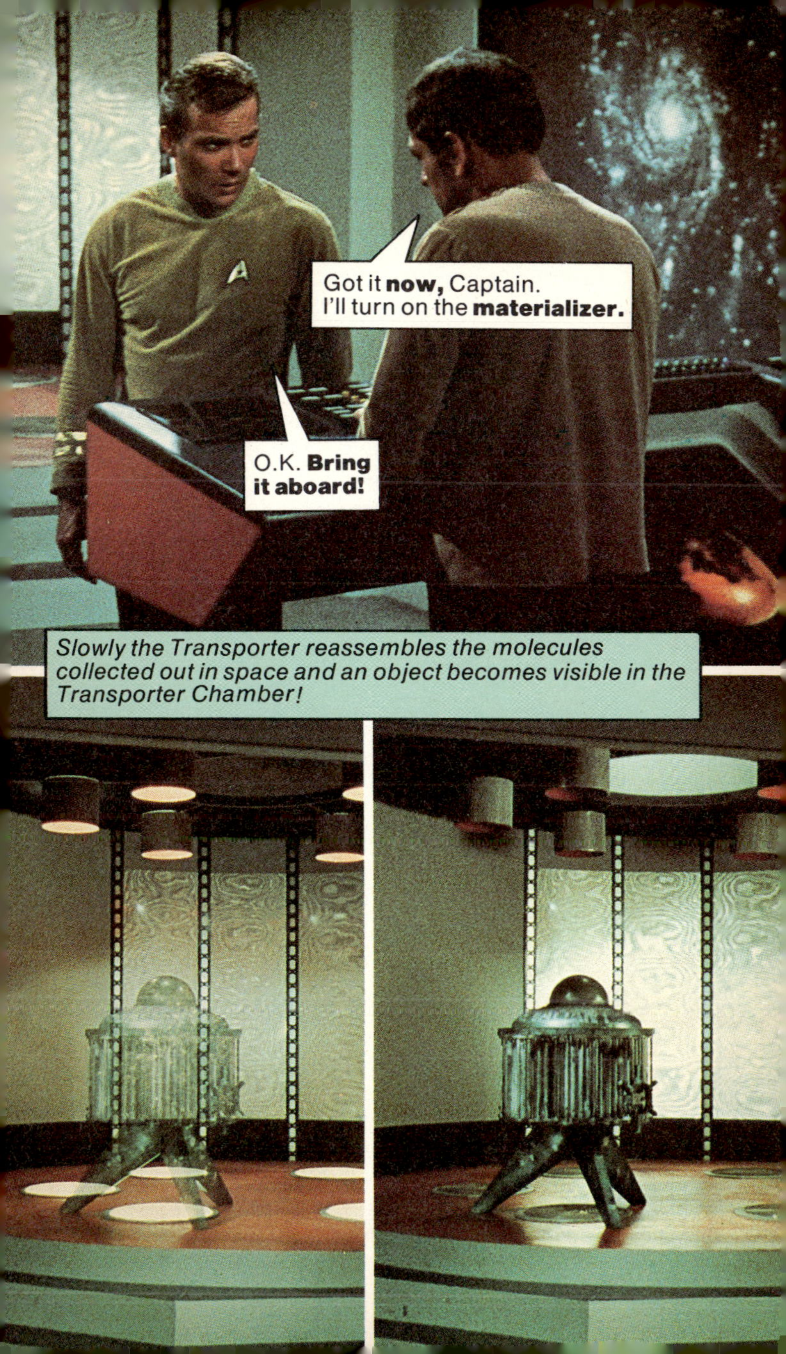
Got it **now,** Captain.
I'll turn on the **materializer.**
O.K. **Bring it aboard!**
Slowly the Transporter reassembles the molecules collected out in space and an object becomes visible in the Transporter Chamber!

It looks like an old-style **ship recorder.** They were made to be **ejectable** when anything threatened the ship.
More like **destroyed** the ship, in this case. Look at it! All **burnt** and **pitted.**
Let's just hope the **tapes** are intact. Scotty, feed them through Mr. Spock's computer.
Yes, sir!

Within seconds of being connected to the computer, the recorder begins transmitting, and soon the data stored long ago will be known. Hopefully it will explain what destroyed the vessel over 200 years ago!
Spock, let's get to the bridge. I'm anxious to see what your computer can make of this. Scotty, flash the bridge. Tell them we're on our way and that I want all department heads to meet me there.

As Kirk and Spock enter the turbolift to go to the bridge . . .
That data should prove **illuminating.**
I certainly **hope** so. We **have** to find out what happened before we leave the galaxy!

In the turbolift they are joined by Kirk's old friend, Lt. Commander Mitchell, who now serves as the ship's Navigator.
Well, Mr. Spock, how did your **chess game** finish up?

The officers arrive on the bridge — the heart of the Starship — and take their places.

Screen on. Approaching galaxy end.
Neutralize warp, Mr. Mitchell, and hold this position.

Yes, sir.

It looks so **peaceful** and yet I feel . . .
I don't see anything out there.
. . . the presence of **something** or **someone.** It's all so incredible! A ship just doesn't **disappear!**
Mitchell, open intercraft communications.
Intercraft communicator open, Captain.

This is the Captain speaking. The object we encountered is a **ship's disaster recorder**, apparently ejected from the **U.S.S. *Valiant*** almost **200 years** ago.
. . . We hope to learn from the recorder what the *Valiant* was doing here . . . what **destroyed** the vessel. We'll move out into our probe as soon as we have those answers. All decks, **stand by.**

Captain, the recorder's tapes are **burned out.** I'm trying the **memory banks** now.

The department heads are reporting now, sir.
Thank you, Mitchell.

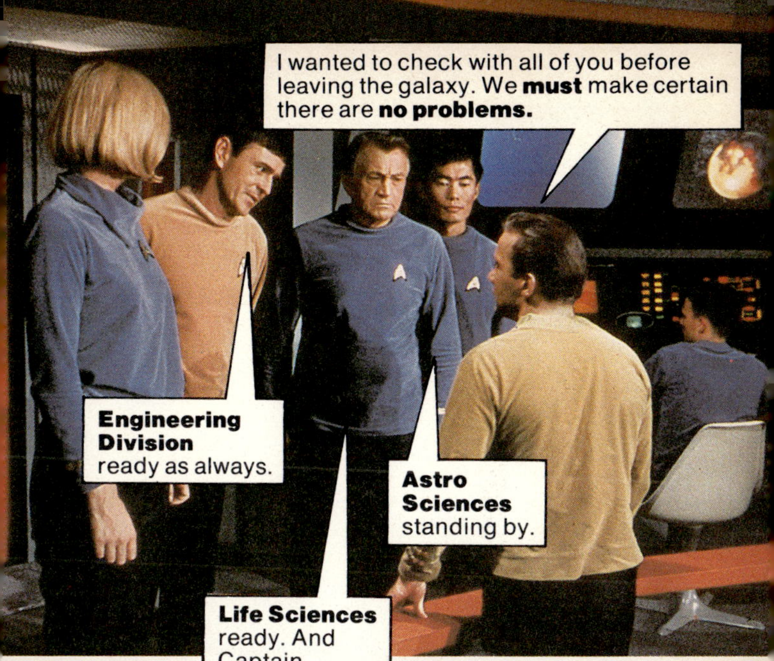
I wanted to check with all of you before leaving the galaxy. We **must** make certain there are **no problems.**
Engineering Division ready as always.
Astro Sciences standing by.
Life Sciences ready. And Captain . . .

. . . This is **Dr. Dehner,** who joined the ship at the Aldebaron Colony.

Immediately Dr. Dehner makes it abundantly clear that she seeks recognition for her professional abilities as a doctor and not for any personal attributes she might possess as an attractive female.
I'm looking forward to working here, Captain. My specialty is psychiatry. My assignment is to study crew reactions in emergency conditions.
But before she can go any further, Spock interrupts.
Captain, I'm getting something from the recorder now!

I'd like to listen to those tapes myself. I'd be **very interested** in how the *Valiant*'s crew reacted to their emergency.
My! My! You **do** take your job **seriously,** don't you?

Improving tho breed, Doctor? Is **that** your line?
I've heard that's more **your** specialty, Commander. **"Line"** included!

After she's gone . . .
Doesn't look like you're going to be able to add **her** to your "list."
Are you kidding? Who needs a **walking freezer unit!**

Meanwhile, Spock has successfully broken through to the recorder's memory banks . . . .
We're decoding now. I'll try to interpolate . . . . It seems that the *Valiant* encountered a **magnetic space storm** and was being swept in this direction . . . .
Those old **impulse engines** they used weren't **strong** enough to break away.

There's more . . . the *Valiant* **passed** this point about a half light year out of the galaxy and then it was **thrown clear** and **turned back!** . . . I'm not getting it all. The tapes are pretty badly burned and it's not coming through very clearly.
But if they **got away** and headed back into the galaxy . . . what **happened** to them?
Wait . . . . It sounds like the ship encountered some **unknown force.**
What **kind** of force? Our sensors haven't picked up **anything.**

. . . Now I'm getting orders . . . now **counterorders** . . . Now I'm getting **repeated requests** for information from the ship's computer records for . . . it's hard to make out . . . for . . . anything concerning **E.S.P. in human beings!**

Kirk, anxious to put the parts of this puzzle together, turns to Dehner for information.
Dr. Dehner, how are you on **E.S.P.?**
In tests I've taken, my E.S.P. rated **rather high.**
Doctor, I'm asking you what you **know** about E.S.P.

Oh, I didn't understand . . . Well, it is a fact that **some** people can **sense** future happenings, read the backs of playing cards and so on. But the **Esper capacity** is always **quite limited.**
More coming through . . There was **severe damage.** Seven crewmen **dead . . . .**
Seven crewmen dead? What does **that** have to do with E.S.P.?

No, make that **six. One** crewman **seemed** to have recovered. **That's** when they became so interested in Extra Sensory Perception. **More** than interested . . . almost **frantic** about it. Wait, this next part is **terribly garbled.**

. . . It sounds like **"Destruct"** . . . I **must** have read it wrong . . . It sounded like the captain giving an order to **destroy his own ship!**
A captain **ordering** his own ship to be destroyed? **Impossible!!!**

But what do the others make of this unbelievable message?
Comments?
The only fact we have **for sure** is that the *Valiant* was **destroyed.**

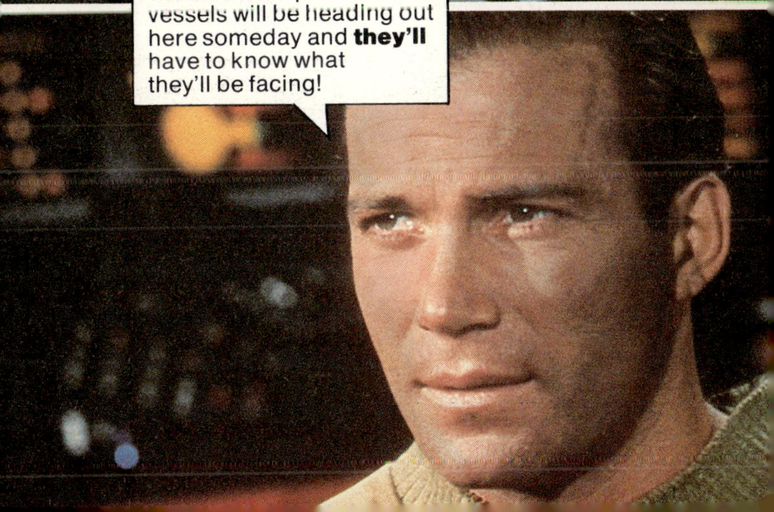
Which is probably the **best** argument to **continue** the probe. Other vessels will be heading out here someday and **they'll** have to know what they'll be facing!

After listening to the others' opinions, Kirk turns his attention back to the screen. He has heard their comments but, as always, the final decision is **his alone** to make.
We're leaving the galaxy, Mr. Mitchell. Ahead warp factor one. **Let's see what's out there.**

Yes, **sir!**

And within **moments** they get their chance!
Captain! What's **that** on the screen?

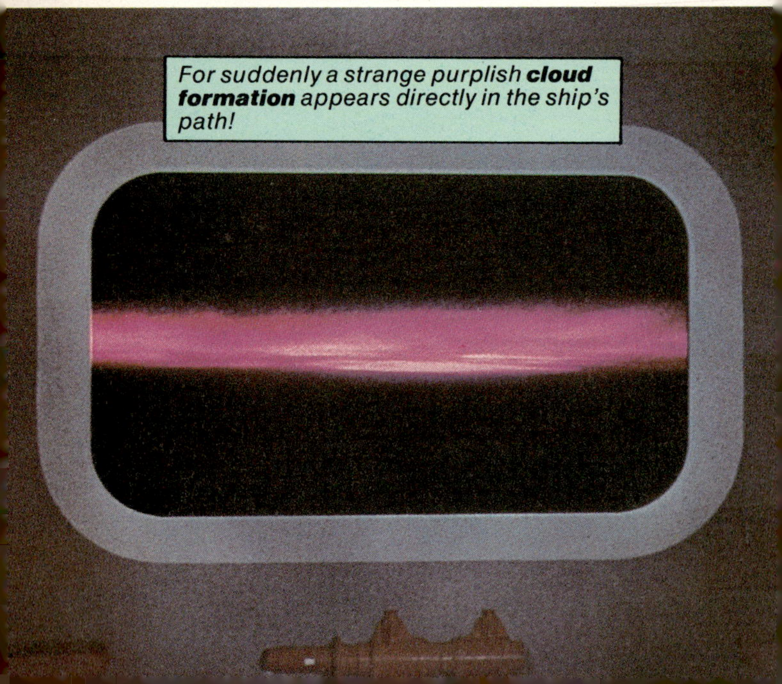
For suddenly a strange purplish **cloud formation** appears directly in the ship's path!

Did the **Valiant's** captain see what **I'm** seeing now? It doesn't **look** so menacing. And yet . . . **six died.** I **heard** the tapes. I've been **warned.** We **still** have time to turn back . . . **no!** We've **got** to find out what that is . . .
Alden, turn sensor beams on and put deflectors at **full** intensity.
Sensor beams now on and deflectors at full intensity, sir.

But even their most modern scientific equipment proves **useless** against this **unknown energy!**
Captain, I'm getting **conflicting reports.** Deflectors say there **is** something there and sensors say there **isn't**. Density: negative. Radiation: negative. Energy: negative.
It must be a **force field** of some kind!

And the Starship glides into the uncharted force field, each crew member anxiously watching the viewscreen ... ***but no one more than their Captain!***

Within **seconds,** the ship is **totally surrounded** by the haze, and the viewscreen is illuminated by a dazzling reddish light that momentarily **blinds** the crew with its **incredible brilliance!** But the blaze of light is not **all** that they have to contend with . . . .

Captain! The instruments . . . they're jammed!!!
As always, with quick calm alertness, Kirk loses no time in responding.
Gravitation on automatic. Emergency stations everyone! All decks on alert!
Kelso, hang in there! Spock — any radiation?

No, Captain.
But the computer is
not responding.
In the next instant
the entire engine
control panel
explodes, sending
sparks and fire
everywhere!

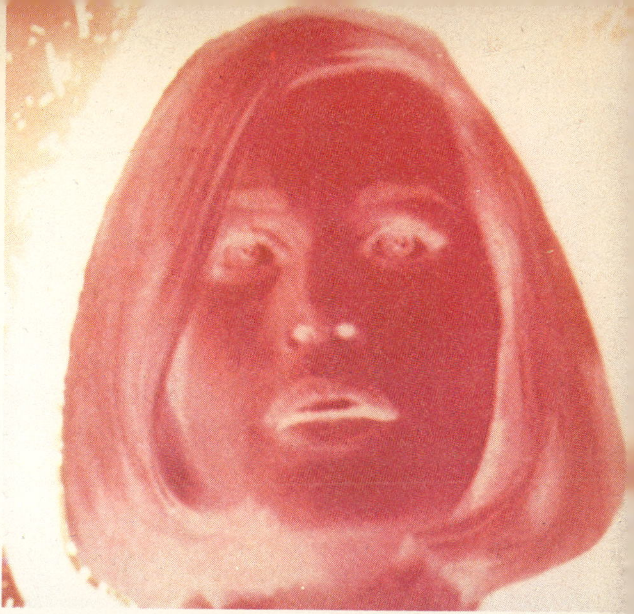

Suddenly, a strange **laser- like beam** flashes through the bridge, singling out Dr. Dehner and Lt. Mitchell with its **searing luminous light!**

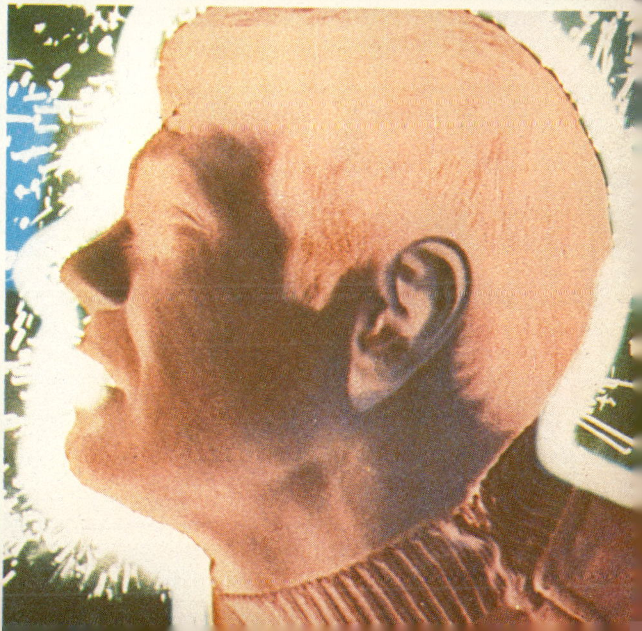

But only for an **instant!** And when it has passed, both **fall to the deck** from the force. Kirk, seeing what has happened, immediately moves to counteract the danger, knowing that his **entire ship's safety** is at stake.

Kelso, neutralize controls — put it on manual — give me lateral power!!
Spock, take over for Mitchell and get us out of here FAST!!

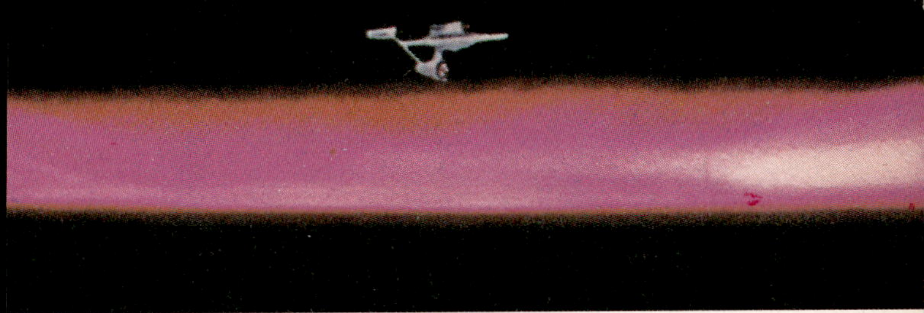

Slowly the ship pulls itself out of the extra-galactic force field . . .

and returns to the safety of the galaxy.

Kelso, take **damage reports.** Spock, find out what that **was.**
Damage control reports — **all** stations.

Dr. Piper — see to Dehner and Mitchell.

*Kirk is **painfully aware** that this encounter with the force field could have been avoided had he **not** ordered his ship out of the galaxy. But the order was made and now they **all** must face the consequences!*
Whatever that flash was **completely knocked out** our engines. We'll have to rely on the **emergency power cells.**
No engines? Those power cells won't last long.

As soon as Kirk is assured that his ship is secured from any imminent danger, he takes a moment to check on the injured crew members.
Something hit me . . . like an **electrical charge.**
She seems to be all right, but I don't know about **Mitchell.** He appears to be in **shock.**

Kirk moves to his friend's side and gently lifts his head . . .
Gary! Are you O.K.?

I'm just a little **weak,** but I feel all right now.
*But it is clear that he is **not all right.** Something is **dreadfully wrong!** His body may feel normal to him but it **isn't.** It **can't** be.*
For normal eyes don't GLOW!!!

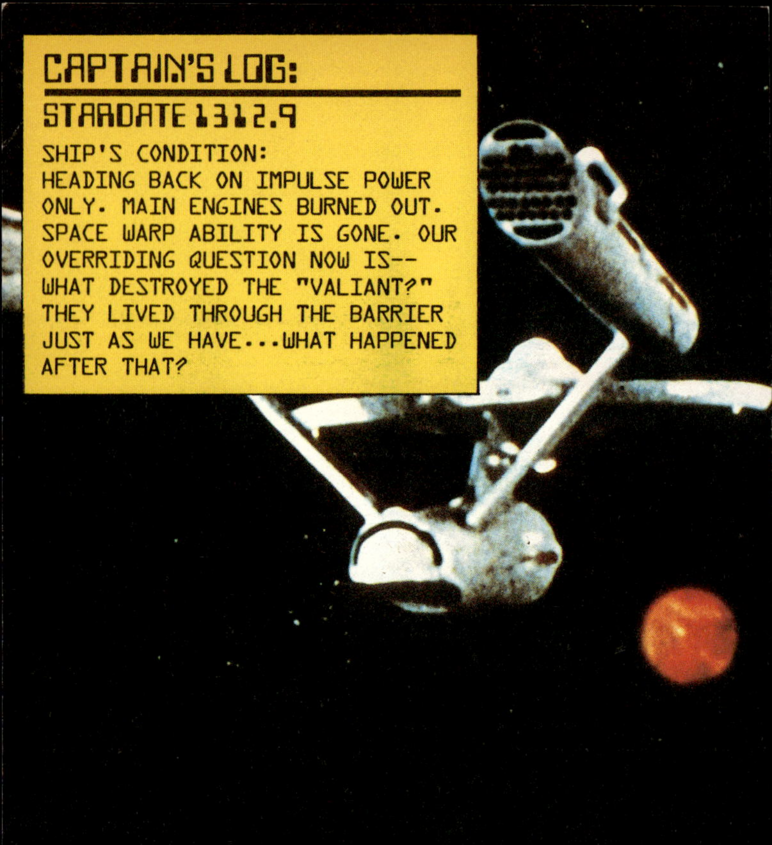
CAPTAIN'S LOG:
STARDATE 1312.9
SHIP'S CONDITION:
HEADING BACK ON IMPULSE POWER ONLY. MAIN ENGINES BURNED OUT. SPACE WARP ABILITY IS GONE. OUR OVERRIDING QUESTION NOW IS-- WHAT DESTROYED THE "VALIANT?" THEY LIVED THROUGH THE BARRIER JUST AS WE HAVE...WHAT HAPPENED AFTER THAT?

Kirk spends the next few hours moving amongst the crew, assessing the damage.
How **bad** is it, Kelso?
I'll know more in a few minutes. But it **doesn't look good!**

ESP RATING

ESPER RATING: 089. APERCEPTION QUOTIENT: 20/100.

DUKE-HEIDELBURG QUOTIENT: 256.

GENERAL KNOWLEDGE QUOTIENT: 654895-109.

ESPER RATING and quotients are better than average in all categories. Subject officer's history indicates an esper orientation pattern since childhood, evidenced in superiority at "guessing games", reading cards et cetera. Esper-orientation and abilities are evident through both the maternal and paternal bloodlines, but in only one case does the indicated tendency toward ESP go back more than three generations.

Subject officer has been aware of the high ESP rating since secondary school days and it is, in part, the basis for interest and vocational training as a psychiatrist. Participation in tests and studies of other esper-oriented beings are the subject of a thesis now being published by this officer in association with the College of Medical Sciences of the Tri-Planetary Academy and was, in fact, the reason for this officer's posting to the Aldebaron Colony.

It must be stressed this officer's interest in esper-perception has been in relationship and pursuant to vocation as a psychiatrist.

As they talk, Dr. Dehner enters the bridge.
Here are the **autopsy reports,** sir. Each case showed damage to the body's **neural circuit**. An area of the brain was **burned out.**
And how are **you** feeling?

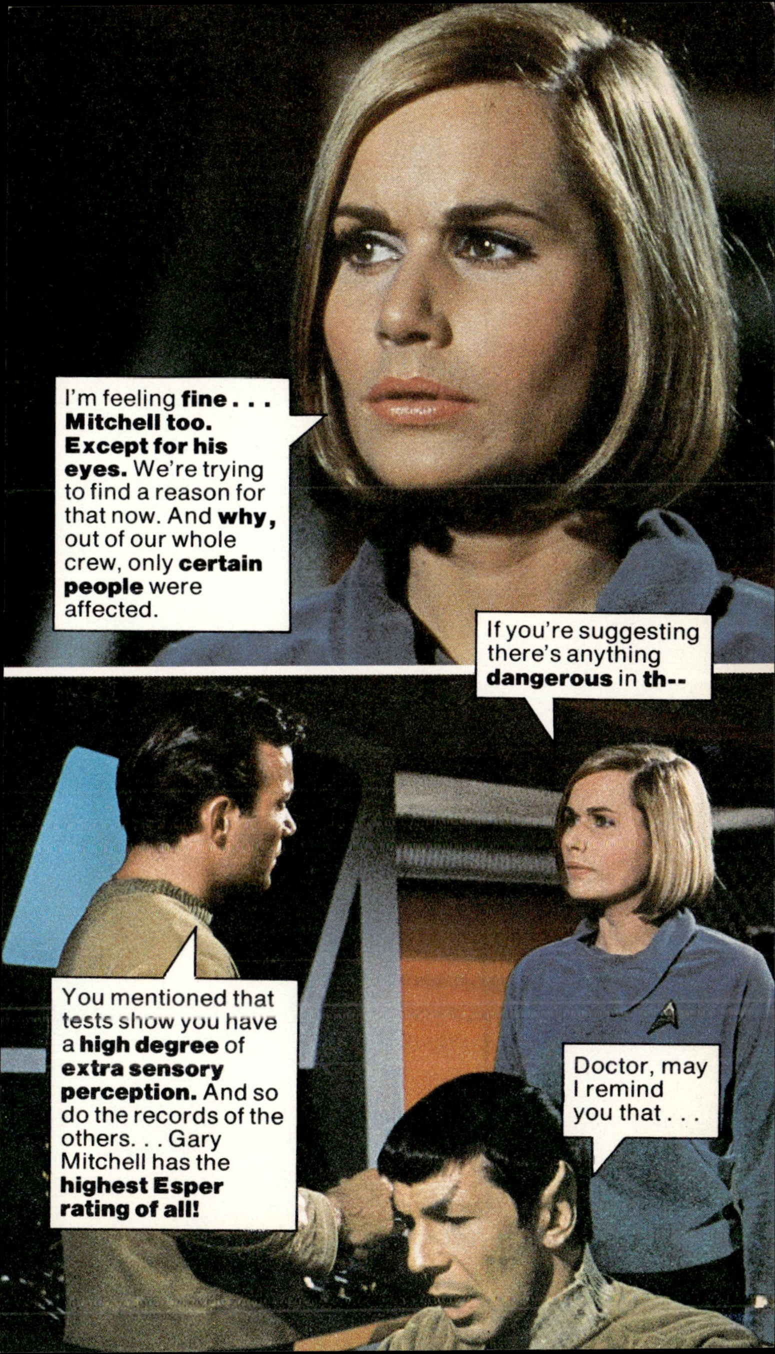
I'm feeling fine . . . Mitchell too. Except for his eyes. We're trying to find a reason for that now. And why, out of our whole crew, only certain people were affected.
If you're suggesting there's anything dangerous in th--
You mentioned that tests show you have a high degree of extra sensory perception. And so do the records of the others. . . Gary Mitchell has the highest Esper rating of all!
Doctor, may I remind you that . . .

. . . before the *Valiant* was destroyed, its captain was **frantically searching** for E.S.P. information on **his** crew?
E.S.P.'s are simply people with **flashes of insight.**
You are talking of **normal** E.S.P. power. But there are **also** those who seem to **see** through solid objects and cause **fires** to start spontaneously.
And you think **we** have people with **that capability** on this ship?

Kirk has raised an ***important question,*** *one that he* ***must*** *find an answer to. For* ***so far*** *the* Enterprise's *voyage has* ***paralled*** *the* Valiant's *and Kirk cannot get the fact out of his head that* ***the Valiant's captain destroyed his own ship!***

The following day Kirk goes down to Sickbay to check on his friend.
Hello, Jim. Good to see you.
That's impossible! How did he know it was me? He's not even looking this way!

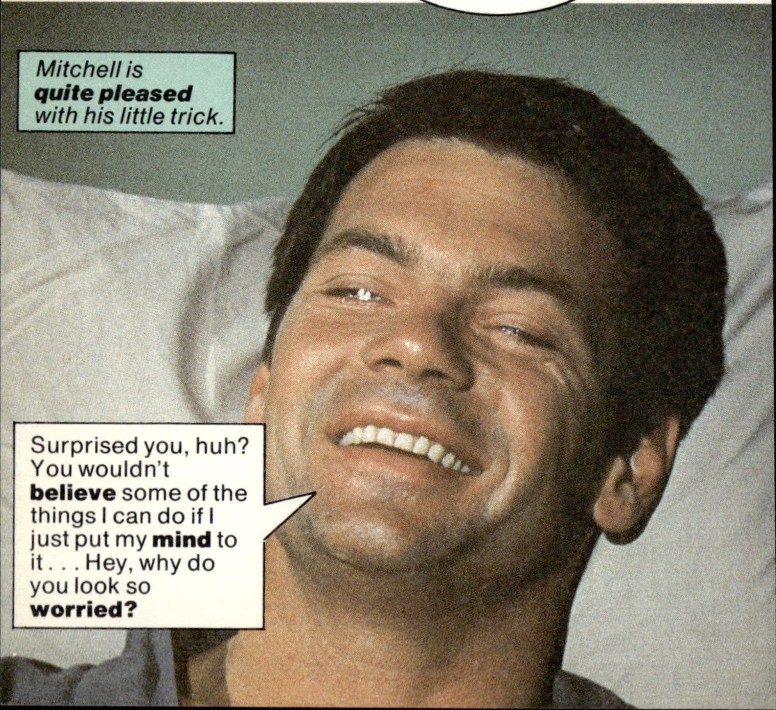
Mitchell is quite pleased with his little trick.
Surprised you, huh? You wouldn't believe some of the things I can do if I just put my mind to it . . . Hey, why do you look so worried?

Worried? Why, I've been worried about **you** ever since that night on Deneb IV. Remember that little **run in** you had with that **attractive brunette?**
Please! Don't remind me. She was **"Nova,"** that one. But don't worry. There's not **nearly** as many after-effects this time. Except for the eyes . . . They kind of **stare back** at me.
How do you feel? Any different?

In a way I feel better than I've ever felt before in my life! It actually seems to have done me some good!
Really? Tell me about it.
Some other time. Right now I want to know when I go back on duty. I'm getting awfully tired of having that iceberg Dr. Dehner hanging around watching my every move.
I think you could use a few more days of rest, Gary. Anyway, you always used to enjoy having an attractive woman around . . . you should consider it a challenge.

Suddenly Mitchell's voice takes on a **strange quality.** It is as if he is speaking from somewhere **out in space** and his voice has **filtered into the ship!**
THAT DOESN'T SOUND VERY **FRIENDLY.** DIDN'T I SAY YOU'D **BETTER** BE **GOOD** TO ME?
Kirk is **stunned** by what he hears, and all traces of friendliness instantly drain from his face!
Listen to **me,** Mitchell! I know we've been friends for a long time, but **never forget** that I'm also **Captain** of this ship . . . **You'll stay here under observation and that is FINAL!**

After Kirk leaves . . .
We'll see, Jim . . . we'll see . . . .

Kirk returns to the bridge, unable to shake premonitions of trouble. There he finds Spock, who has also sensed the strange new attitude in Lt. Mitchell and has been monitoring the Sickbay's viewscreen.
Look at that, Captain. He's reading even faster now than just a few minutes ago!
He's already gone through half of the ship's library tapes today.

Is that the Gary Mitchell you **used to know?**
No, it **isn't. Something** has definitely happened to him . . . . Put a 24-hour watch on the Sickbay and order the **fullest possible range** of examinations and tests.
Order what you want, Captain . . . **it won't make any difference!**

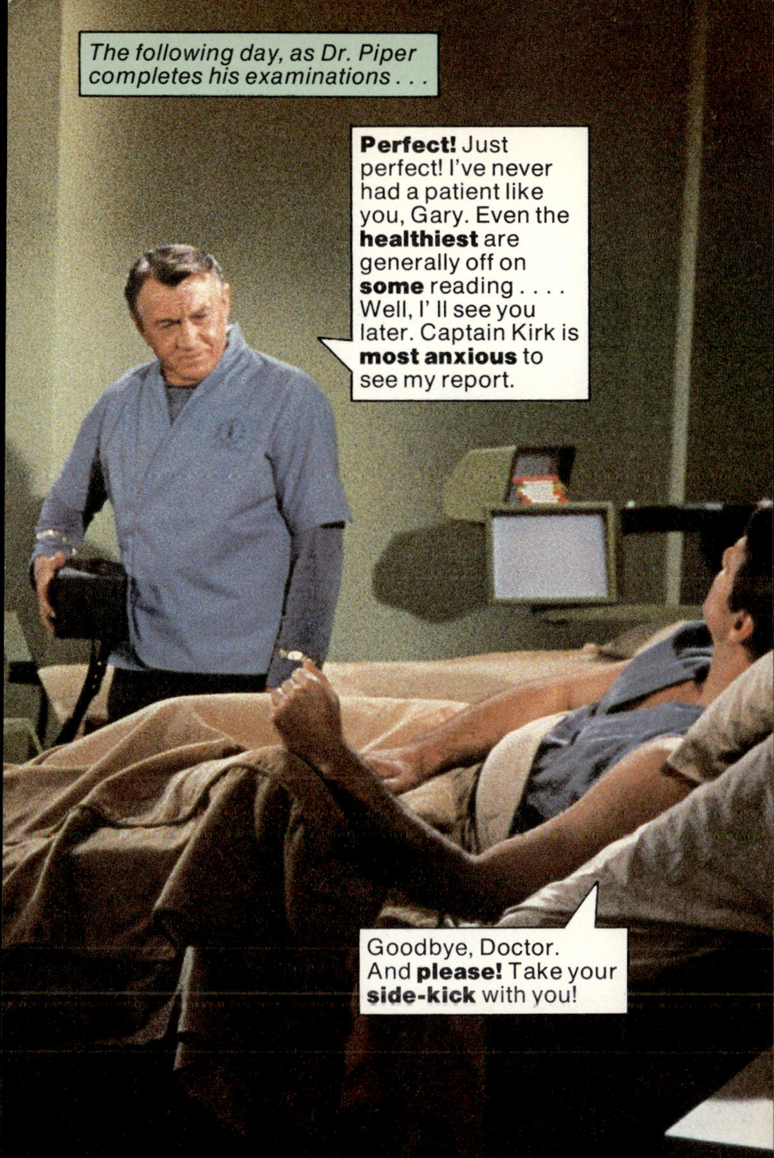
The following day, as Dr. Piper completes his examinations . . .
Perfect! Just perfect! I've never had a patient like you, Gary. Even the healthiest are generally off on some reading . . . . Well, I' ll see you later. Captain Kirk is most anxious to see my report.
Goodbye, Doctor. And please! Take your side-kick with you!

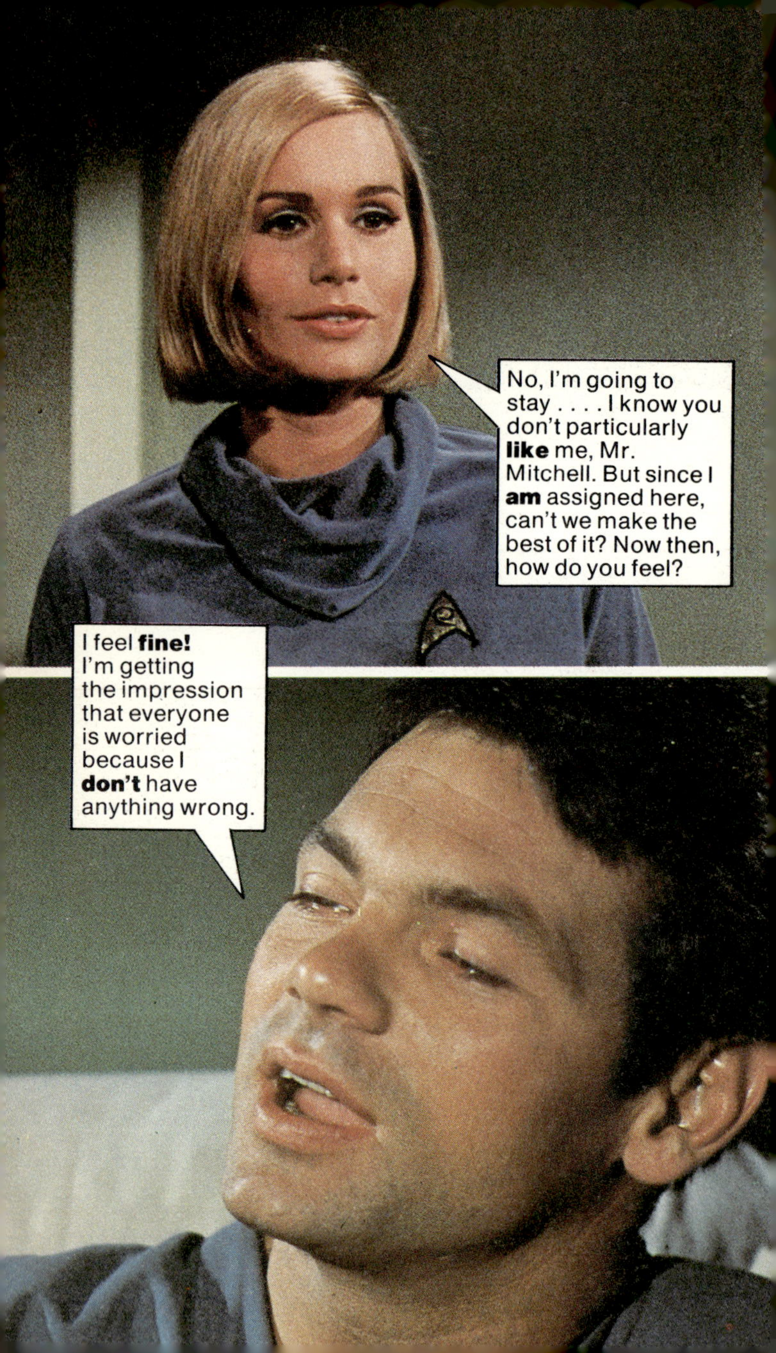
No, I'm going to stay . . . . I know you don't particularly **like** me, Mr. Mitchell. But since I **am** assigned here, can't we make the best of it? Now then, how do you feel?
I feel **fine!** I'm getting the impression that everyone is worried because I **don't** have anything wrong.

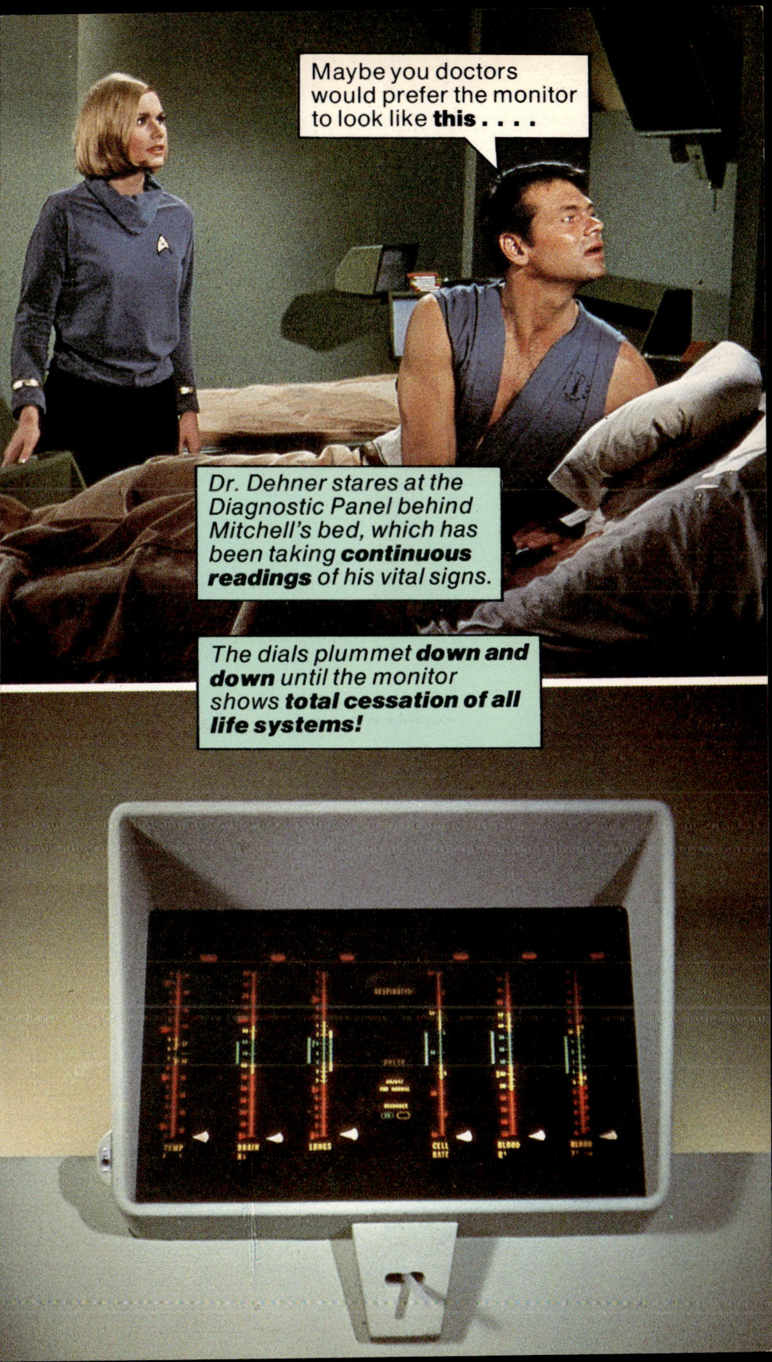
Maybe you doctors would prefer the monitor to look like **this . . . .**
Dr. Dehner stares at the Diagnostic Panel behind Mitchell's bed, which has been taking ***continuous readings*** *of his vital signs.*
The dials plummet ***down and down*** *until the monitor shows* ***total cessation of all life systems!***

What **happened?** He **can't** be **dead!** It's **impossible . . .** we were **just talking!** But the monitor?
There's **no pulse!**
Gary! Do you hear me?
Slowly a ***mischievous smile*** *appears on Mitchell's face.*
Sure, doll! I hear you **loud and clear!**

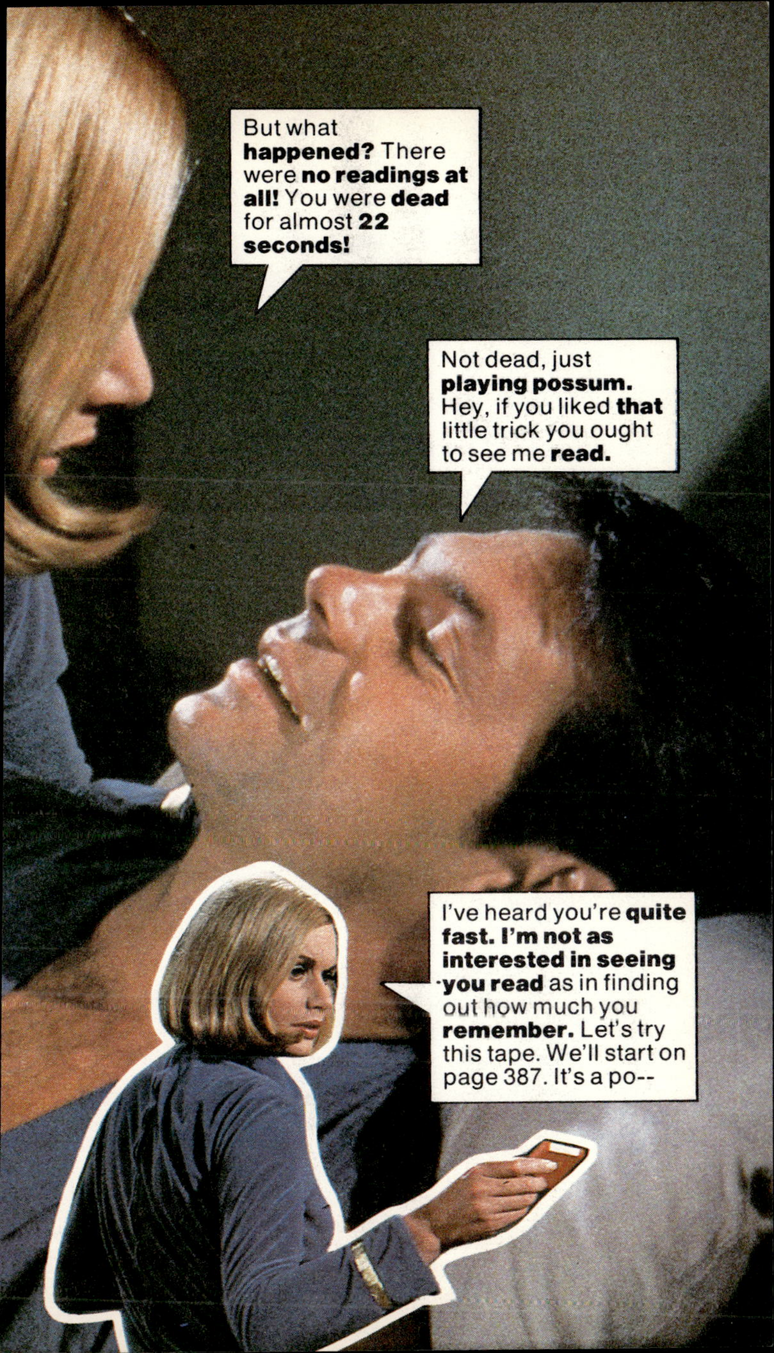

But what **happened?** There were **no readings at all!** You were **dead** for almost **22 seconds!**
Not dead, just **playing possum.** Hey, if you liked **that** little trick you ought to see me **read.**
I've heard you're **quite fast. I'm not as interested in seeing you read** as in finding out how much you **remember.** Let's try this tape. We'll start on page 387. It's a po--

Yes, I **know** what it is— a very **touching** poem . . . .
"My love has wings, slendered feathered things. With grace in upswept curves and tapered tip."
It's called "The Nightingale Woman," written by Tarbolde on a Canopus planet back in 1996.
You said that **beautifully!**
It's funny you chose **that** one. It's one of the **most passionate love sonnets** of the past few centuries. In some ways it captures my thoughts about **y--**

But before he can finish, Kelso comes into the room.
Oh, **excuse me.** I . . . I was just on my coffee break and . . . oh . . . I thought I'd **check up** on . . . eh . . .

Hey, that's **O.K.,** Lee. Come on in . . . and stop looking at me so **funny.** Don't let the **light** in my eyes bother you, pal. It's all for our good looking **lady doctor** here.
Sure . . . .

So, how go the **repairs?**
Well, the main engines are gone and unless we can find someway to **re-energize** them, it looks like we're **stuck** here.

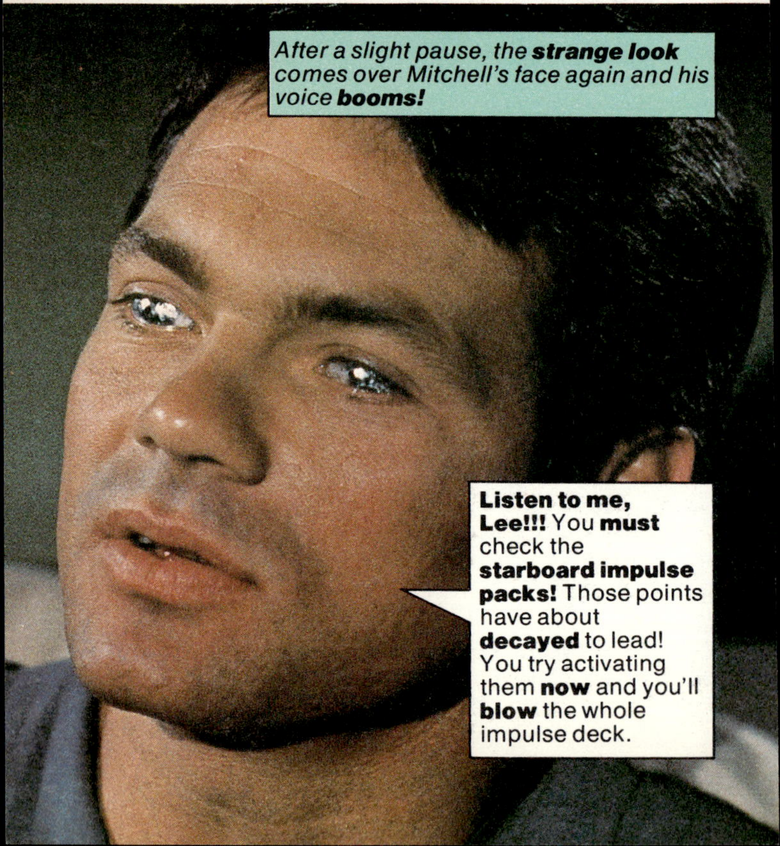
*After a slight pause, the **strange look** comes over Mitchell's face again and his voice **booms!***
Listen to me, Lee!!! You **must** check the **starboard impulse packs!** Those points have about **decayed** to lead! You try activating them **now** and you'll **blow** the whole impulse deck.

Who does he think he's talking to that way? He's got to be **nuts!** And those **eyes.** I'm getting **out** of here!
Well, I've got to get back to the bridge. Thanks for the suggestion . . . I'll see you later!

After Kelso has left, Elizabeth turns to Mitchell, full of wonderment.
How did you know **that? You** haven't checked the impulse packs!
I didn't **have** to. **He** did. And the **image** of what he'd seen **was still in his mind!**

That afternoon Capt. Kirk calls an emergency meeting of his chief crew members. All day he has been receiving incredible reports concerning Mitchell's behavior, not the least of which he has just been hearing from Kelso.
. . . and you say you took this from the starboard impulse pack, Kelso?
Yes, sir. It just didn't make any sense that **Mitchell** would know, but he sounded so **sure** that I decided to check the circuits anyway. I **couldn't believe it!** He was **absolutely right!** This point was burned out **exactly** the way he described it.

As Kelso finishes, Dr. Dehner joins the others in the briefing room.
Sorry I'm late. I became so interested in observing **Gary** . . . eh . . . I mean **Mr. Mitchell**--
Dr. Dehner, our subject is **not** Gary Mitchell. Our concern **is,** rather, what he is **mutating** into.

I know those from your planet aren't **supposed** to have feelings like **we** do, Mr. Spock. But to talk that way about a man you've worked next to for years is **worse** than ev--
That's **enough,** doctor!
I don't think so! I understand **you** least of all, Captain. Gary told me that you've been friends since he joined the service . . . that you even **asked** for him aboard your first command.

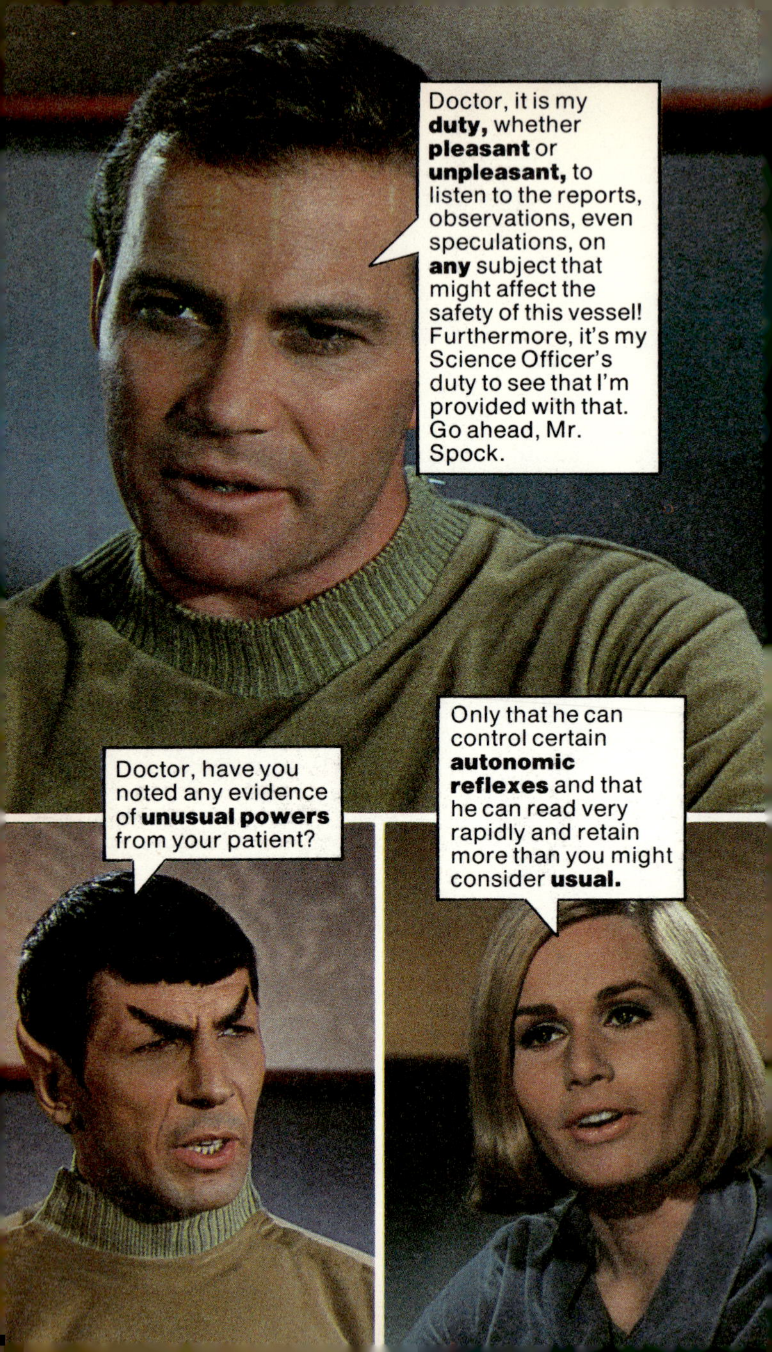
Doctor, it is my **duty,** whether **pleasant** or **unpleasant,** to listen to the reports, observations, even speculations, on **any** subject that might affect the safety of this vessel! Furthermore, it's my Science Officer's duty to see that I'm provided with that. Go ahead, Mr. Spock.
Doctor, have you noted any evidence of **unusual powers** from your patient?
Only that he can control certain **autonomic reflexes** and that he can read very rapidly and retain more than you might consider **usual.**

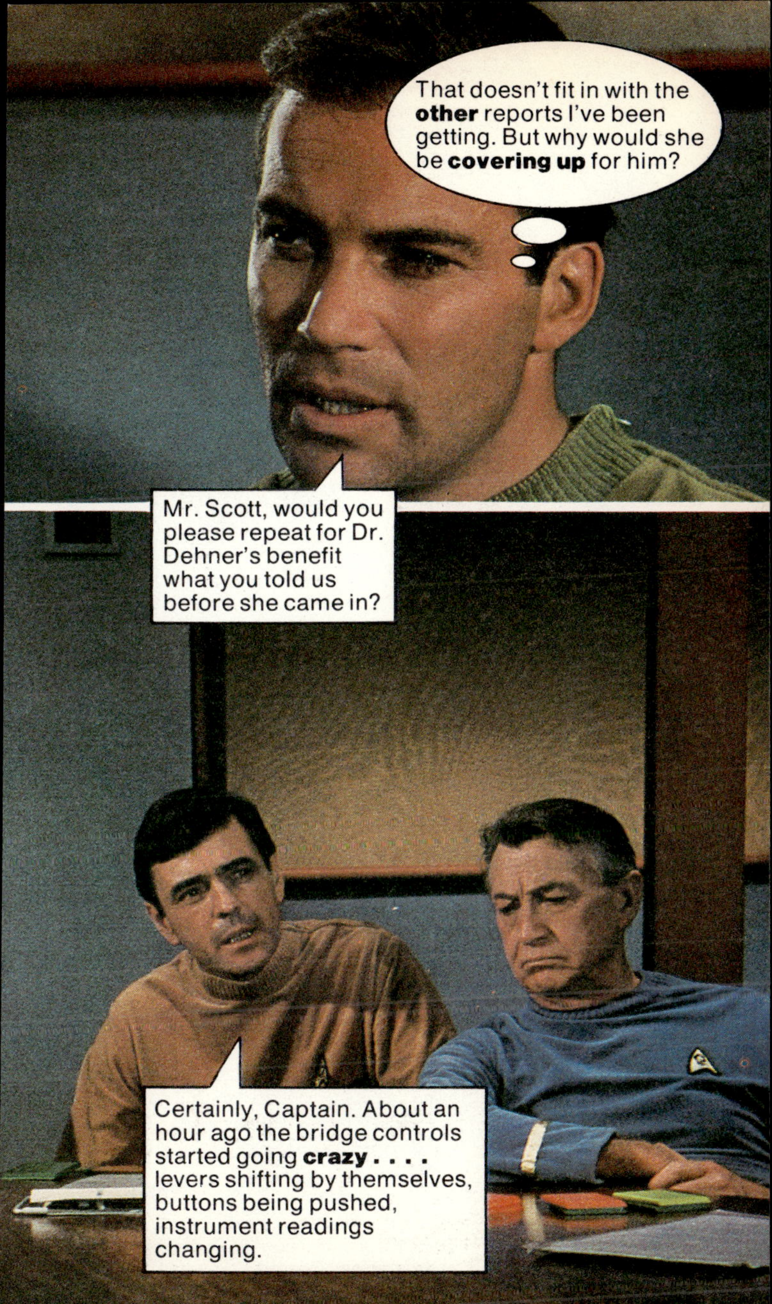
That doesn't fit in with the **other** reports I've been getting. But why would she be **covering up** for him?
Mr. Scott, would you please repeat for Dr. Dehner's benefit what you told us before she came in?
Certainly, Captain. About an hour ago the bridge controls started going **crazy** . . . . levers shifting by themselves, buttons being pushed, instrument readings changing.

And on my monitor screen I could see Mitchell **smiling** each time it happened. It was as if this entire ship and crew were almost a **toy** for his amusement!
Are they **right,** Doctor? **Has** he shown abilities of such magnitude?
*Elizabeth hesitates in answering, knowing that her words will have **great bearing** on their discussion.*
I . . . eh . . . saw **some** such indications.

Exploding with fury, Kirk counters.
And you didn't think it worth mentioning?

No one's been hurt, have they? Don't you understand? A mutated superior man could also be a wonderful thing . . . a forerunner of a new and better kind of human being!

Kirk weighs all that he has heard. He knows only too well that any decision he makes will affect every person aboard the starship. But what decision should he make? After a few moments he turns his attention to Mr. Sulu, hoping that he can add something.
Mr. Sulu? Any comments?
If you want the **mathematics** of this, Captain, Mitchell's ability is increasing **geometrically. That** is like having a penny and **doubling** it every day. In a month you'd be a **millionaire.**
In less time than that, Mitchell will have attained powers we **can't** understand and **won't** be able to **cope** with. Soon each person on this vessel will not only be useless to him, but will actually be an **annoyance.**

Kirk has heard enough.
I thank **each** of you for your input. I want **no** discussion of any of this with the crew. As soon as I have made a decision I will notify you. You're dismissed.

As the others leave, Spock stays behind. He senses Kirk's indecision and feels that Kirk is wasting ***precious time.***
Jim, you **must** realize that we'll **never** reach an Earth base with Mitchell aboard. You heard the mathematics of it. In a month he'll have as much in common with us as we'd have with a ship full of **white mice!**
What I need are **recommendations,** Spock, **not** vague warnings!
Certainly, Captain. Recommendation Number 1: There's a planet a few light days away from here — **Delta-Vega.** It has a lithium cracking station. We may be able to adapt some of its **power packs** to our engines.
And if we can't, we'll be **trapped** in orbit there. You realize, of course, that we haven't enough power to blast back out.

It's the **only** possible way to get Mitchell off this ship!

If you mean **strand** Mitchell there, I **won't do it.** The station is fully automated — there's not a soul on the whole planet. Even the ore ships call only **once every 20 years!**

You have **one** other choice — **kill** Mitchell while you still can. It is your **only** alternative, assuming you make it while you still have time!
Will you **try** for **one moment** to **feel?** At least **act** like you've got a heart! . . . or have you forgotten we're talking about Gary?
The captain of the *Valiant* probably felt the same way. And he waited **too long** to make his decision. I think we've **both** guessed that by now.
Left alone, Kirk goes over again all that he has heard. But no matter how many times he reviews the facts, only ***one*** *possible solution crosses his mind. Even though his profound respect for all human life* ***rebels*** *at the very thought, he knows he can not escape from his duty. There* ***is*** *no alternative.*
Gary . . . . forgive me.

CAPTAIN'S LOG:

STARDATE 1313.1

WE ARE NOW APPROACHING DELTA-VEGA. OUR COURSE IS SET FOR A STANDARD ORBIT. THIS PLANET, COMPLETELY UNINHABITED, IS SLIGHTLY SMALLER THAN EARTH--DESOLATE BUT RICH IN CRYSTAL AND MINERALS. KELSO'S TASK: TRANSPORT DOWN WITH A REPAIR PARTY AND TRY TO REGENERATE THE MAIN ENGINES AND SAVE THE SHIP. OUR TASK IS TO TRANSPORT DOWN A MAN I'VE KNOWN FOR 15 YEARS. AND, IF WE'RE SUCCESSFUL, MAROON HIM THERE.

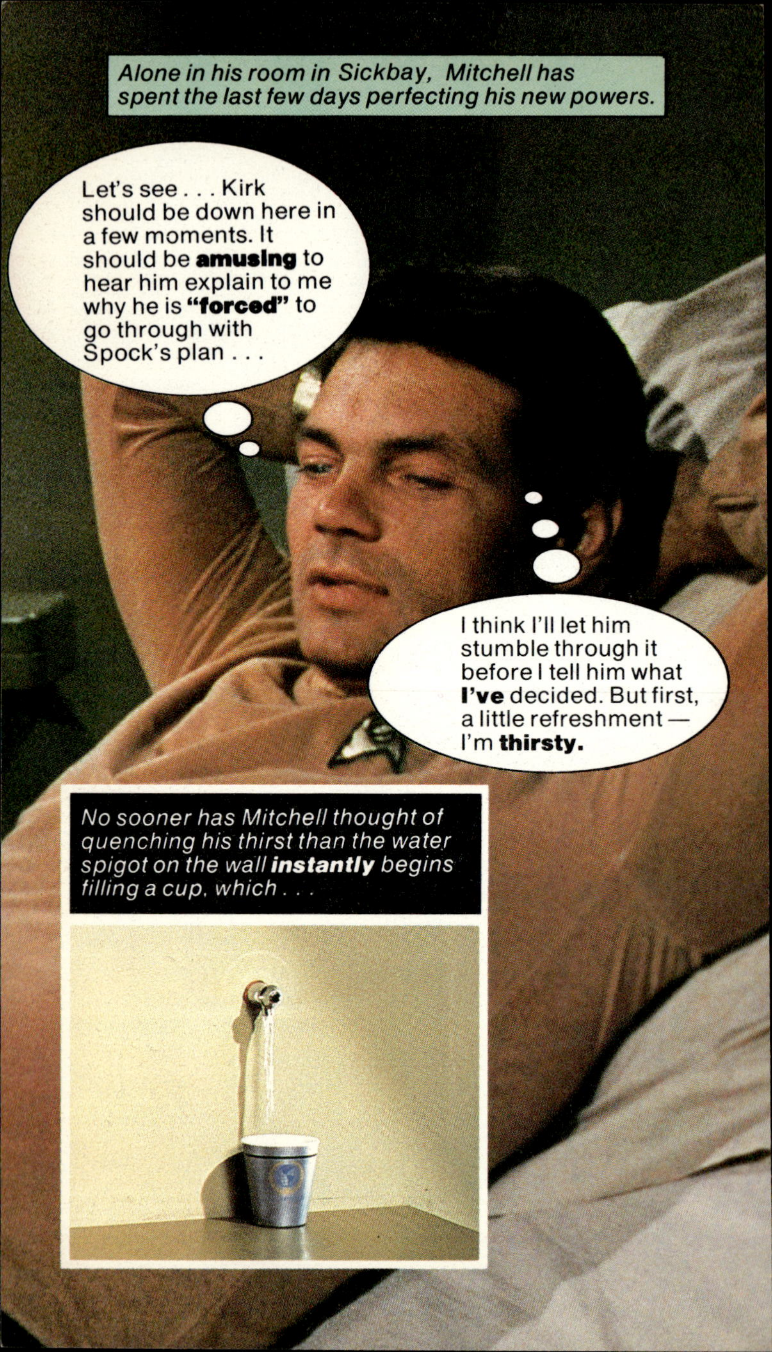

Alone in his room in Sickbay, Mitchell has spent the last few days perfecting his new powers.
Let's see . . . Kirk should be down here in a few moments. It should be amusing to hear him explain to me why he is "forced" to go through with Spock's plan . . .
I think I'll let him stumble through it before I tell him what I've decided. But first, a little refreshment — I'm thirsty.
No sooner has Mitchell thought of quenching his thirst than the water spigot on the wall instantly begins filling a cup, which . . .

. . . then floats across the room, **directly into Mitchell's waiting hand!** Captain Kirk, entering just ahead of Dr. Dehner and Spock, is a shocked witness to all.
Come in! Come in! The **floor show** is just finishing.
You know, it's like a man who has been **blind** all of his life who has suddenly been given sight . . . Sometimes I feel that there's **nothing** I couldn't do, in time. Some people think that makes me a **monster, don't they, Jim?**
It is **worse** than I thought! We may not be able to even get him off the ship!

Are you reading **all** our thoughts, Gary?
Actually, I can **sense** them. And I can sense mainly **worry** in you Jim — concern about the safety of your ship.
And as Mitchell playfully sends the cup into Kirk's hand, the others watch with amazement.
That's **quite** a trick, Gary, but we have more **serious** business to discuss. I want to know what **you** would do in **my** place.

I? What would I do? . . . . Probably just what Mr. Spock is thinking right now. Kill me while you can!
You see no alternatives?
You seem to have it backwards. You are the one with no alternatives, not me!

Without warning, Mitchell raises his hand and emits a **powerful shock wave** that hurls Kirk across the room.
Gary! STOP IT!!!
AHHH . . . OWWW!

Stay back, Jim.
I warn you!!!

Stop **what?** I know we're orbiting Delta-Vega and I **can't** let you force me down there. I may not want to leave this ship . . . not **yet.** I may want **another** place. I'm not sure yet just what kind of a world I can **use.**
Use? What's **happening** to you? What **are** you talking about?
I don't understand it all yet. But if I keep **growing . . . getting stronger** . . . why, the things I could do . . . like maybe a **god** could do.

While Mitchell's attention is momentarily turned to Elizabeth, Kirk sees his chance and lunges at him, throwing his ***entire body*** into Mitchell's side! The swiftness of Kirk's movement catches Mitchell off guard and ***for a moment*** he is overpowered!

Quickly, Spock and Kirk carry Mitchell to the bed.
Doctor! Give him a sedative, **fast!** I want him unconscious for a while. We've got to be able to **control** him.

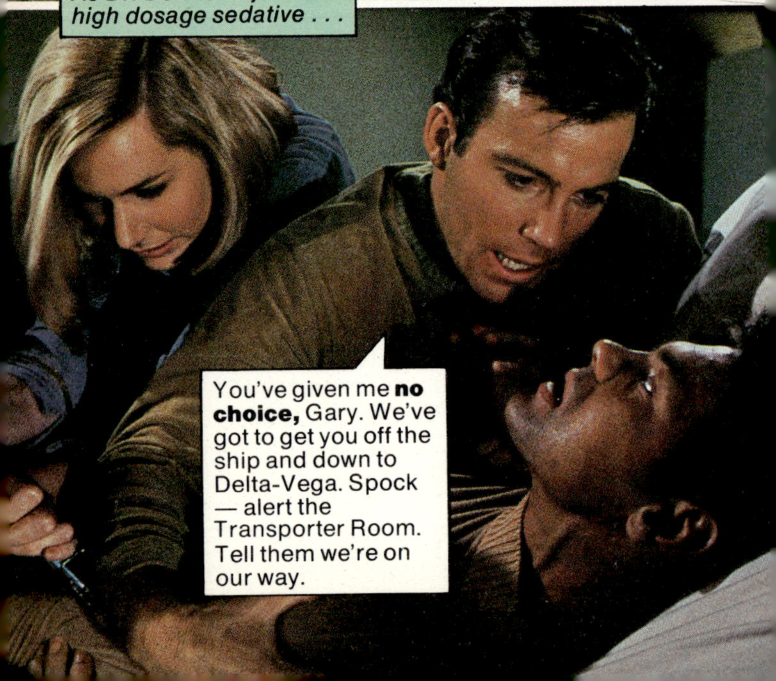
As Dr. Dehner injects a high dosage sedative . . .
You've given me **no choice,** Gary. We've got to get you off the ship and down to Delta-Vega. Spock — alert the Transporter Room. Tell them we're on our way.

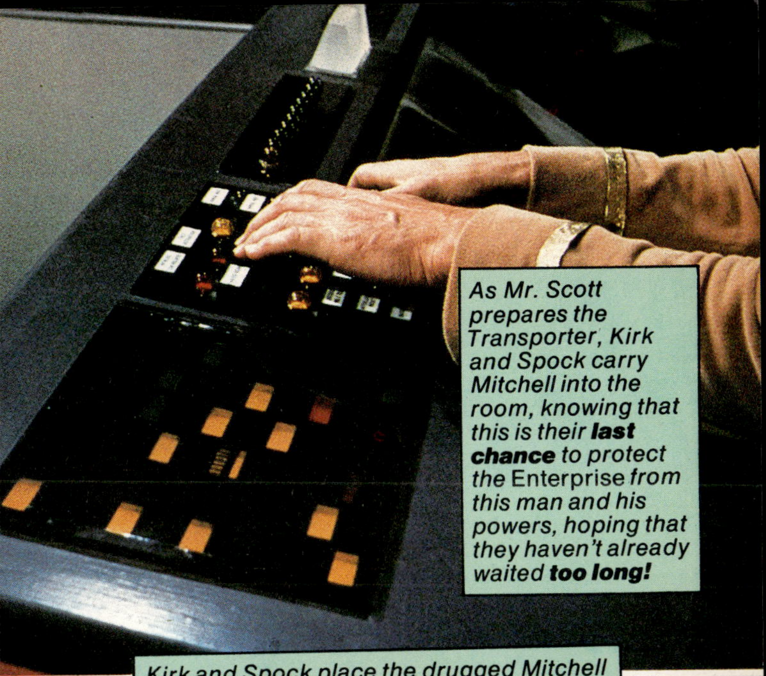
As Mr. Scott prepares the Transporter, Kirk and Spock carry Mitchell into the room, knowing that this is their **last chance** to protect the Enterprise from this man and his powers, hoping that they haven't already waited **too long!**

Kirk and Spock place the drugged Mitchell in the Transporter Chamber.
Be **careful** with him, Captain.
Hurry, Spock! Kelso and his crew are already down there. **We have no time to lose!**

Just then the tranquilizer wears off!
YOU FOOLS!! Soon I'll SQUASH you like INSECTS!!!
Doctor — give him another shot. We can't hold him much longer!
The transporter is ready if you are, Captain.

The landing party is beamed down to Delta-Vega. Seconds later they materialize. But even Dr. Piper's most potent drugs have no lasting effect.
Mitchell begins to regain consciousness as Kelso and members of his repair crew come to meet the landing party.
Spock — take him in and find an appropriate place to keep him. Kelso, are you going to be able to regenerate the ship's engines?
Maybe, if we can bypass the fuel bins without **blowing ourselves up!**

Mitchell is taken away. Kirk and Dr. Dehner now get their first **real** look at the desolate planet!
Incredible!!

There's not a **soul** on this planet but **us.**
Nobody but us **chickens,** Doctor.
But Kirk is only trying to hide his true feelings. As he looks out at the barren landscape, ***totally*** *devoid of human life, his heart is* ***torn*** *when he thinks that this is where his friend will be spending* ***the rest of his life!***

But Mitchell is not Kirk's **only** concern. His ship hovers **helplessly** overhead and he must find a way to repair its engines. Entering the Control Station, he is immediately briefed on the repair crew's progress.
We've got the 203-R set, sir.
Good. Let's hope it works on the ship. Transport it up.
We need to have the fuel bins detonated from here. What about rigging up a **destruct switch?**
I guess I could wire one to this panel.
Captain, Mitchell has **completely** regained consciousness.

Mitchell is being kept in a small room. In its doorway is a high voltage force field that emits a near lethal shock wave if any object breaks its continuous flow.
Dr. Piper, I want only one medical officer here at any one time. The other will monitor Mitchell on the dispensary screen.
I'd like to stay now. Maybe I'll be able to talk to him.

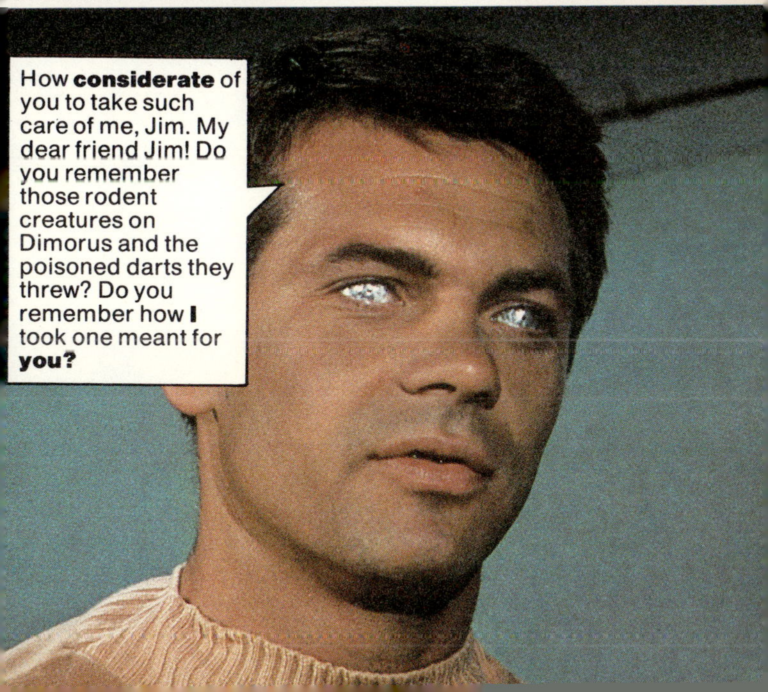
How considerate of you to take such care of me, Jim. My dear friend Jim! Do you remember those rodent creatures on Dimorus and the poisoned darts they threw? Do you remember how I took one meant for you?

How **could** I forget? you almost **died!**
*Kirk remembers **only too well!** He hasn't been able to forget **many** things about their friendship, which makes what he has to do all the more painful. Painful, yes, but nevertheless**,** **unavoidable.** For he would **never** allow **anything** or **anyone** to endanger his ship.*

So why be afraid of me now?

Because you've been **testing** your ability to take over the *Enterprise*. In the transporter you said something about us seeming like **insects** by comparison. You said you'd **squash** us if we got in your way.

And in the Sickbay you said if you were in **my** place, you'd **kill** a mutant like yourself.

Then why **don't** you kill me? Mr. Spock is **right** and you are a **fool** if you can't see it. Man cannot survive if a race of **true Espers** is born. In time you'll understand.
As Mitchell speaks he moves to the doorway and tries to pass through. But the force field is immediately activated and his powers are unable to counteract the shock waves!
Get back! GET BACK!
Gary! Stop it!
*Mitchell's body is thrown back into the room by the force! For a moment he is **totally immobilized.***

Is he **dying?**
No. Fighting the force field has temporarily drained his strength. He can be handled now.

Is that **possible?** Gary? **Are you O.K. again?**
*Slowly Mitchell's eyes return to **normal!***

But in a few moments the strange glow returns, and now it is **even brighter and more penetrating!**
You'll regret this . . . I'll just keep getting stronger. You **know** that, don't you? **I'll just keep getting stronger!**

High above Delta-Vega, the Enterprise *is* ***locked in orbit!***

Scott is working **feverishly,** connecting the makeshift equipment salvaged from the planet to the ship's complex engineering circuitry.
Communicator, report to the captain that it **fits like a glove!**
Meanwhile, back on the planet . . .
Spock, why are you carrying that **phaser rifle?**
Mitchell tried to get through the force field again and . . .

. . . this time his eyes changed back **faster** and he didn't become as weak.
The untenable strain of having his friend's life in his hands begins to show.
Dr. Dehner feels he isn't **that** dangerous. What makes **you** right and a **trained psychiatrist** wrong?

Because she **"feels."** I **don't.** All I know is **logic** and in my opinion we'll be lucky if we can repair this ship and get away in time!

As Kirk thinks over Spock's warning . . .
The destruct switch is connected, Captain — direct to the power bins.
All right, Kelso. I want you to stay here. If Mitchell gets out, at your discretion, if you think you're the last chance — **I want you to hit that button.**

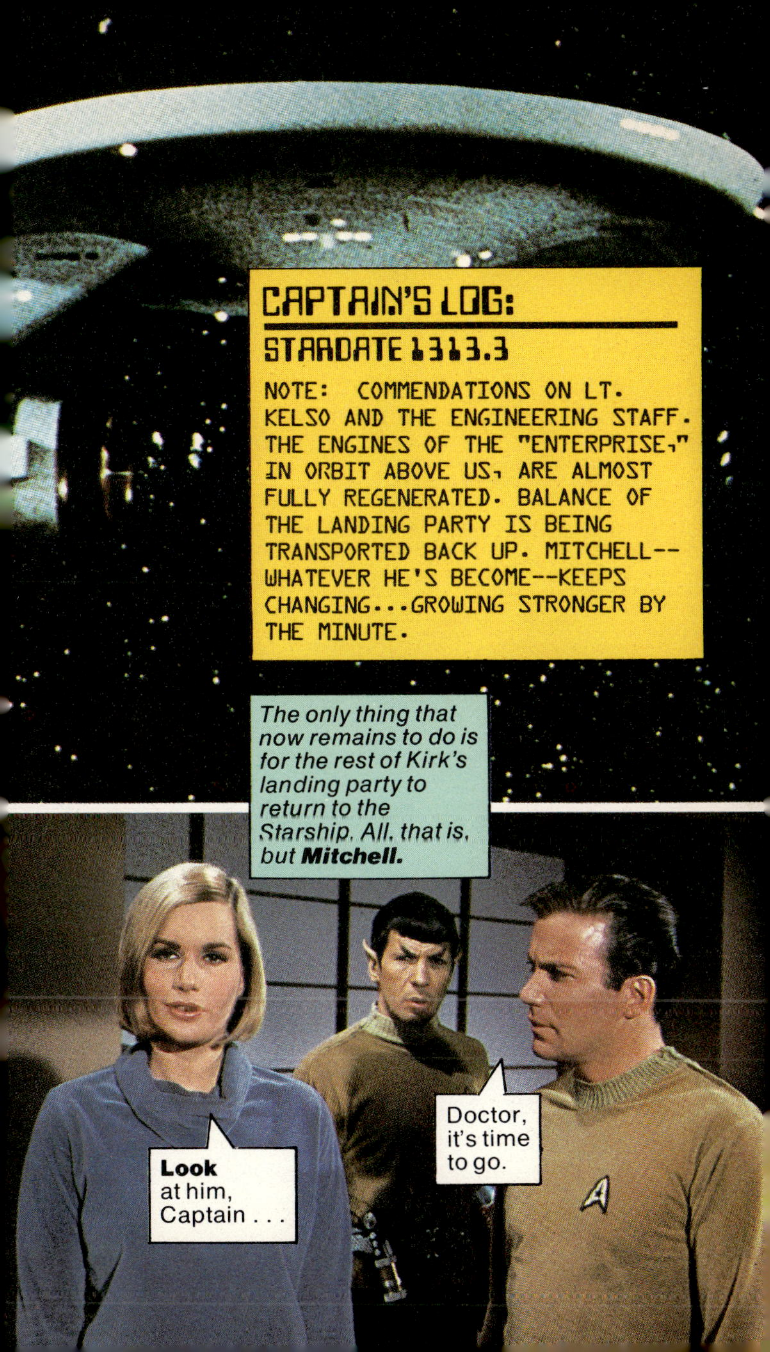

CAPTAIN'S LOG:
STARDATE 1313.3
NOTE: COMMENDATIONS ON LT. KELSO AND THE ENGINEERING STAFF. THE ENGINES OF THE "ENTERPRISE," IN ORBIT ABOVE US, ARE ALMOST FULLY REGENERATED. BALANCE OF THE LANDING PARTY IS BEING TRANSPORTED BACK UP. MITCHELL--WHATEVER HE'S BECOME--KEEPS CHANGING...GROWING STRONGER BY THE MINUTE.
The only thing that now remains to do is for the rest of Kirk's landing party to return to the Starship. All, that is, but ***Mitchell.***
Look at him, Captain . . .
Doctor, it's time to go.

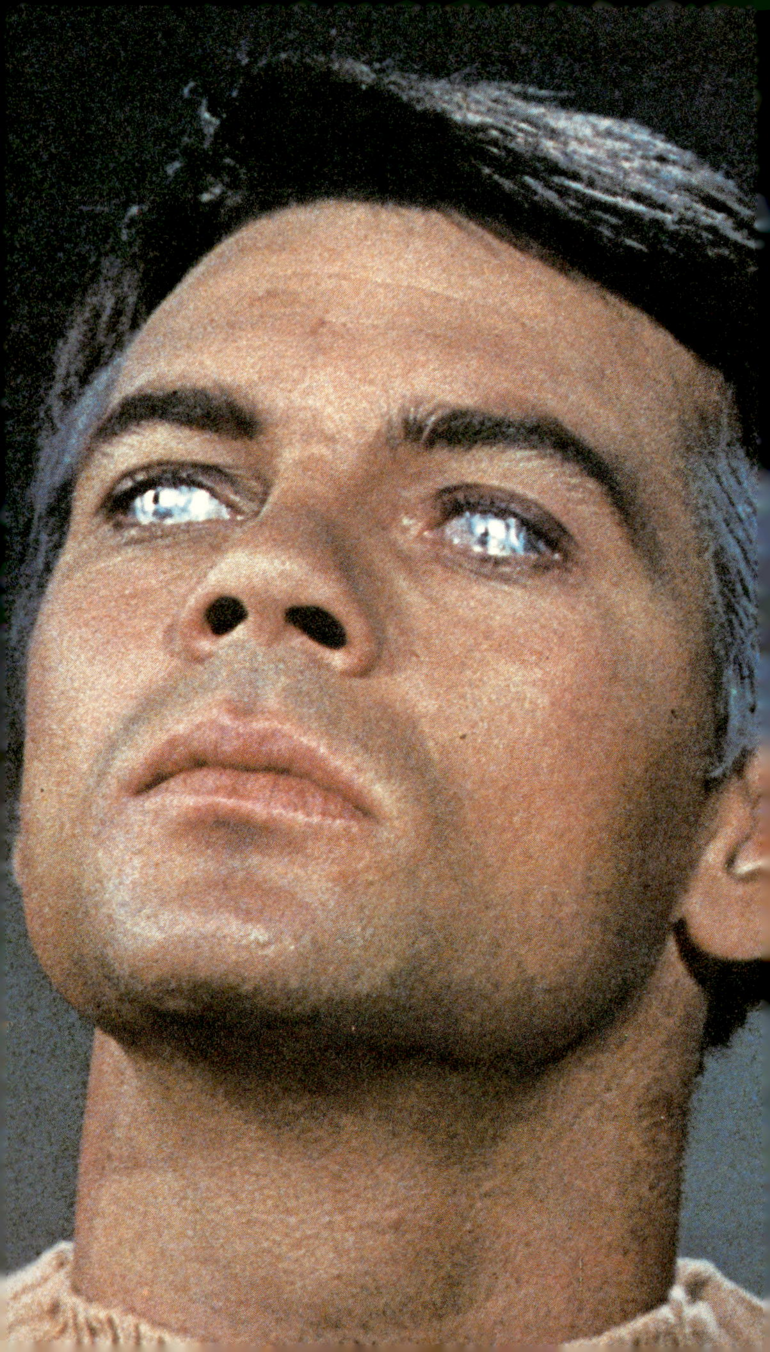

. . . . He's been like that for **hours.**
What can he be **thinking** about?
Spock, have Dr. Piper meet us in the Control Room with Kelso. We'll all transport up together.
And if Mitchell should try to stop us?
Kelso will be on the destruct button until the **last minute . . .** I think Gary, **knows** that.
Captain, I'm **staying behind** with him!
That's **out of the question,** Dr. Dehner.

Mitchell certainly ***does*** *know the Captain's plans, but he has plans of his own, and they will* ***not*** *be thwarted! For that very moment he is concentrating all his thoughts on an unsuspecting Kelso, who is sending in his final report to Mr. Scott on the* **Starship.**
Fission chamber checks out. The station seems to be running **perfectly.**
Move, cables . . . **move . . . .**
You're a **talented thief,** Kelso. Everything you sent up is fitting in place.
I must admit, Mr. Scott, I'm kind of **proud** of the job. We're preparing . . .

But Kelso will **never** finish his report. For Mitchell is using all his powers to move the heavy cables **higher and higher!** And like a **huge sinewy snake** it inches its way up **until** . . .
KILL!!! KILL!!!
Stop . . . Oh . . . No . . . Ugh . . . ehhh . . . AAAHHH!!
The cable coils itself around Kelso's neck and **tightens and tightens** itself, pulling the **very life** out of him!

Totally unaware *of what has just occurred, Kirk continues to talk to the doctor.*
You just don't **understand** Gary. He's not **evil.**
I will **not** debate this with you **any further.** You're leaving with us, Doctor, and **that's an order!!!**
Just a minute, James. **No one** is giving any orders around here but **me!** You know, you **should** have killed me while you **could.** Command and compassion is a **fool's mixture.**
And as he finishes he raises his hand and sends a powerful ***repelling force*** *directly at Kirk!*

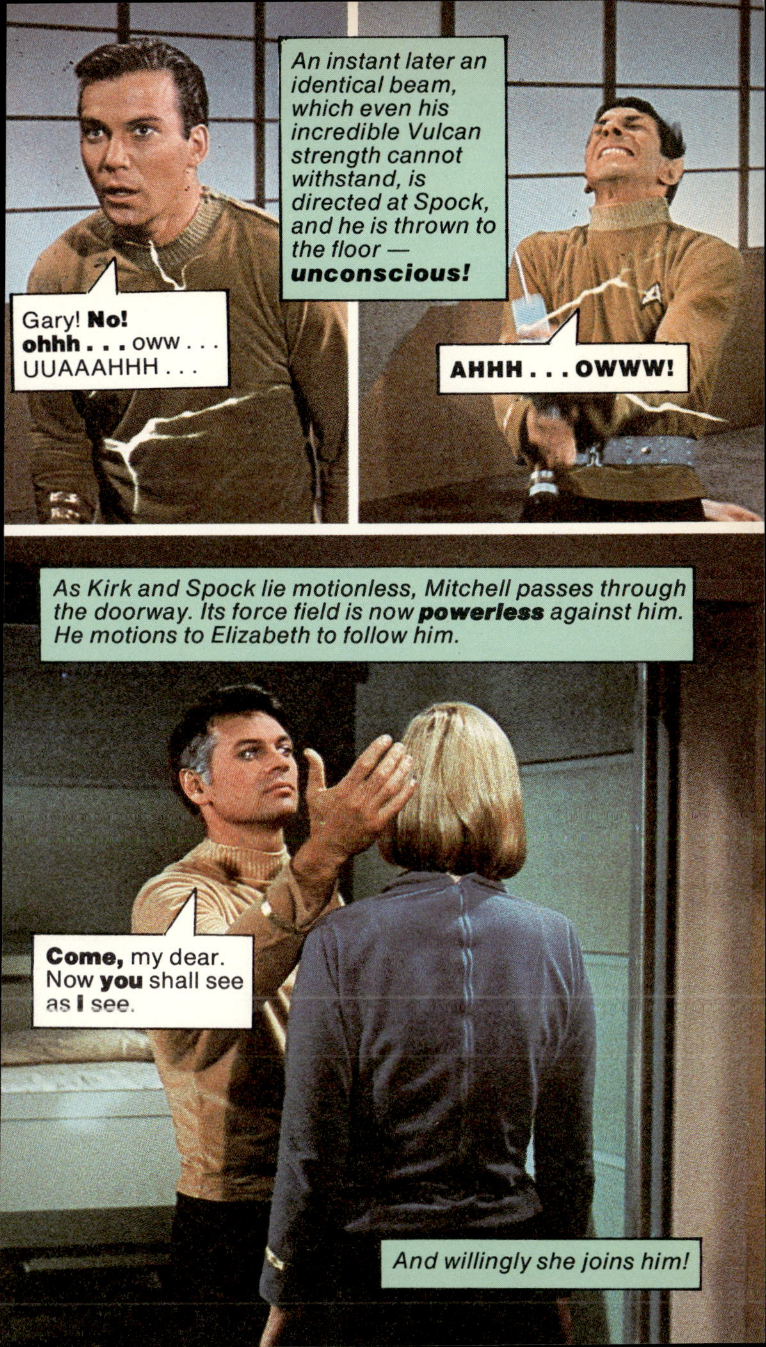
Gary! No! ohhh . . . oww . . . UUAAAHHH . . .
An instant later an identical beam, which even his incredible Vulcan strength cannot withstand, is directed at Spock, and he is thrown to the floor — unconscious!
AHHH . . . OWWW!
As Kirk and Spock lie motionless, Mitchell passes through the doorway. Its force field is now powerless against him. He motions to Elizabeth to follow him.
Come, my dear. Now you shall see as I see.
And willingly she joins him!

For though it took longer to affect her, the strange force that entered her body when she was hit by the charge on the bridge has finally begun to take over!
Nothing can stop us now. You are as I am. We are the same.
We are as ONE.

Having seen all that has happened over the dispensary's viewer, Dr. Piper rushes to Kirk and Spock.
Just lay there for a second, Captain. I think Spock got it worse than you.

Will he be all right?
I think so. Here, take one of these pills. You'll feel better in a few moments . . . I wish I could say the same for Kelso. I passed through the control room . . . There's no easy way to say this — Kelso's **dead — strangled!**
Oh **no!** And Dr. Dehner? Is **she** all right?
I'm not sure. She went with Mitchell. They headed across the valley to the left of the pointed peaks. There are flatlands beyond.
Kirk grabs the phaser rifle, knowing what he must do.
Don't give Spock a pill until **after** I'm gone. It's **my** fault Mitchell got as far as he did. When Spock recovers, you'll both transport up **immediately** to the *Enterprise*.
But Captain . . .
No "buts," Doctor! If you haven't received a signal from me in 12 hours, proceed at **maximum warp** to the nearest Earth base with my recommendation that this **entire planet** be subject to a lethal concentration of **neutron radiation!** No protest on this, Mark. **That's an order!!!**

Not far away, Mitchell and Elizabeth have been exploring their new "home." As far as they can see, it is a panorama of craggy rocks and boulders.
Look at this, Gary. It would take a **miracle** to survive here.
Then **I** shall **make** one.

*For Mitchell has the power to **create** as well as **destroy.***
Behold, Elizabeth — **a miracle . . .**
And with a movement of his hand . . .

Where once was just sand and dust, a beautiful garden — an ***Eden*** *— appears . . .*

. . . full of magnificent flowers and lush foliage with a trickling brook running through the rich soil — a place ***fit for a god!***

It's beautiful . . . **absolutely beautiful!. . .**
Come . . .

All of this is **ours . . .** We shall make a **paradise!**
You'll soon share this feeling, Elizabeth . . . **to be like a god . . .** to have the power to make this world **anything you want it to be!**
*But what **does** Mitchell want his world to be? A place of **beauty** and **fulfillment,** or a place where he can carry on his reign of **terror** and **destruction?***

But Mitchell will **not** have such control if Kirk can help it. Not knowing that Elizabeth has joined Mitchell willingly, he has been tracking them and at that very moment he is approaching their "paradise."
I feel someone is near.
I do too. We are soon to have a visitor . . . **a very foolish man.**
Kirk is not a **foolish** man, but a **desperate** man, as he slowly makes his way through the jagged boulders and rocks.

You'll **enjoy** being a god, Elizabeth. Let us nourish ourselves while we wait. Come . . . let us eat.
*And **instantly** a plant pushes itself through the rich soil, and in its foliage are **succulent fruits.***
Kaferian apples — **fit for the gods!**
Unaware that his approach is being closely monitored, Kirk creeps cautiously, edging his way to Elizabeth and Mitchell.
There's **nothing** I can do for Mitchell. It's **too late.** But I **must** save the doctor . . . It's **my** fault that things have gone this far. If I can just catch Mitchell **off guard . . .**

But Kirk is dreadfully underestimating Mitchell's powers . . .
Have some, my dear, before our **guest** arrives. He's getting **closer.**
Suddenly Kirk hears Mitchell's voice coming from he knows not where!

James? Can you **hear** me? No, you can't **see** me. I'm not **there . . .**
Just follow the **right** path and you'll come to me **soon.**
I can see him in my mind too.
Go to him, Elizabeth . . . . **Talk** to him. Now that you're changing, I want you to see just how unimportant **"they"** are.

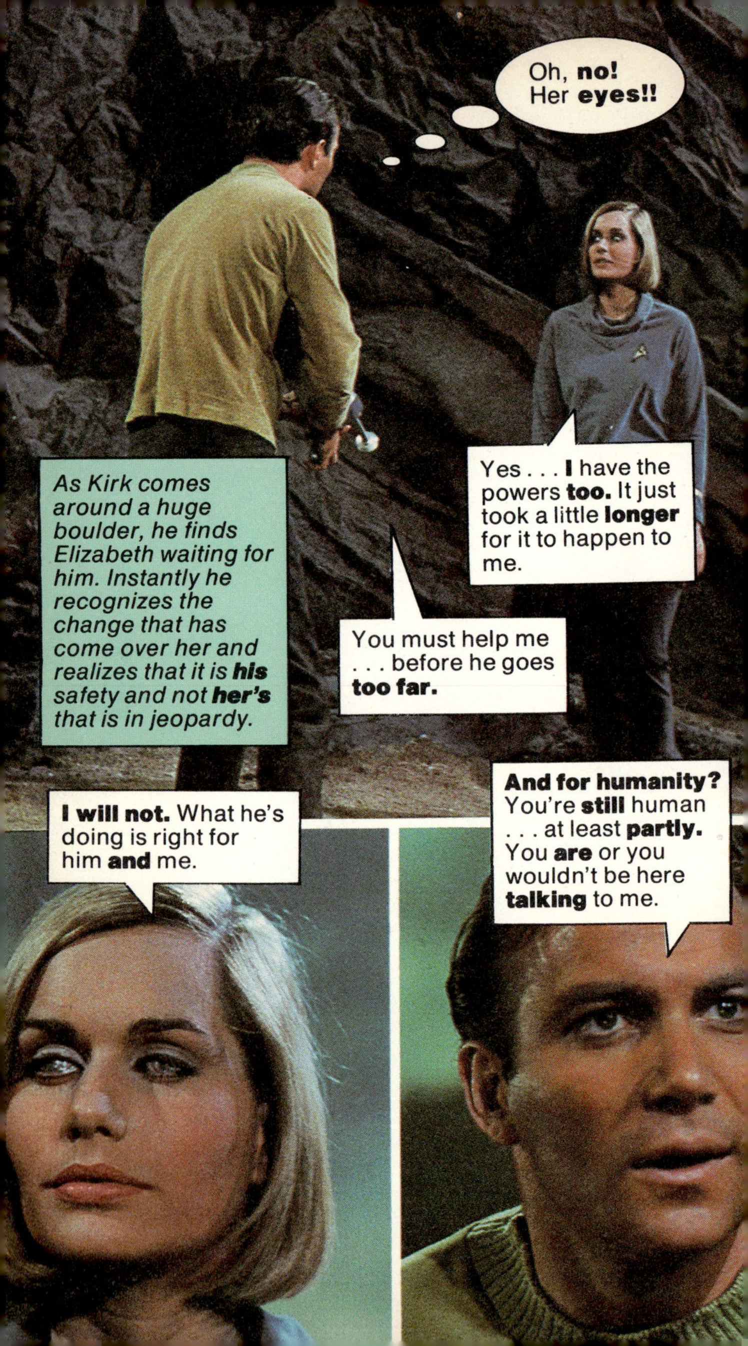
Oh, no! Her eyes!!
As Kirk comes around a huge boulder, he finds Elizabeth waiting for him. Instantly he recognizes the change that has come over her and realizes that it is his safety and not her's that is in jeopardy.
Yes . . . I have the powers too. It just took a little longer for it to happen to me.
You must help me . . . before he goes too far.
I will not. What he's doing is right for him and me.
And for humanity? You're still human . . . at least partly. You are or you wouldn't be here talking to me.

Please! Go back while you still can! Earth is really unimportant to us. Before long we'll be where it would have taken mankind millions of years of learning to reach.
And what kind of world will he create? Will he know what to do with his power? Will he acquire wisdom?
Knowing that he needs Elizabeth on his side, Kirk presses his point.
Did you hear him joke about compassion? Above all else, a god needs compassion!
What do you know about gods?

Then let's talk about **humans** . . . about our **frailties.** As powerful as he gets, he'll still have all **that** inside of him.
I've warned you! GO BACK!!

Listen to me! You were a psychiatrist once. You know the ugly, savage things we all keep buried . . . that none of us dare expose. But he'll dare. Who's to stop him? He doesn't need to care . . . Be a psychiatrist for one minute longer. What do you see happening to him? What's your prognosis, doctor?
I've warned you. Now it's too late. He's coming.
Then watch him. Hang on to being a human for one minute longer. Come on, Mitchell . . . I'm ready for you.
I'm disappointed in you, Elizabeth. But not in you, Jim. Predictably dedicated to the end!

Desperately Kirk aims the phaser rifle at Mitchell . . .

. . . unleashing its full force **directly at his heart!**

But it is of **no use!** Man's weapons have no effect on a **"god."**
A fighter 'till the **very end.** Your crew would have been **proud!**
And with a gesture of Mitchell's arm, the rifle pulls itself out of Kirk's hands and flies through the air!

I've been contemplating the **death** of an old friend and I've decided that you deserve a **decent burial,** at least.
Do you think **that** spot would make a nice grave?
And with a motion of his hand . . .

. . . while Kirk stares in horror, a deep hole appears in the ground and Kirk confronts his **own tombstone!**
JAMES R. KIRK

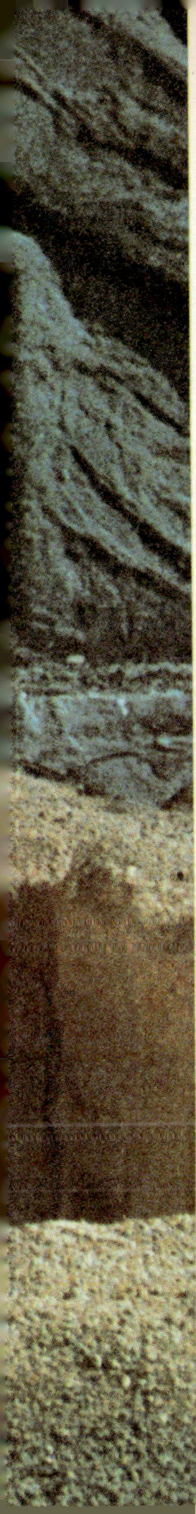

Suddenly an enormous boulder is pulled loose from the mountain side and begins to fall, down to where Kirk is.

But as it falls, Elizabeth yells out . . .

And just as quickly as the boulder began to move, it stops!
You shouldn't have done that, Elizabeth. Morals are for men, not gods!
A god . . . but still driven by human frailty. Doctor, do you like what you see?
Elizabeth stands motionless. No! She does not like what she sees. She does not like the way Mitchell's mind has been affected by his powers. She does not like what she now realizes he is capable of doing . . .

You **shall** die, Captain. But not **yet.** First you will **pray** to me. Pray that you die **easily!**
And once again Mitchell raises his hand . . .

. . . this time sending an excruciating force that pushes Kirk back no matter how hard he tries to resist!
Pray to **you,** Mitchell? Not to **both** of you??? **Uuaaahhhhh . . . .**

Enough! I shall hear no more!
And another piercing, agonizing pain rips through Kirk, pushing him to his knees!
AAAHHH!!!

He'll **kill** him! He's **dying** in front of my eyes! **No!** I **can't** let it happen!
Gary! **Stop!** You **must** not do this!
Doctor, **look** at him and you'll know that in the end there will be only **one** of you. **Only one.** One **jealous god.** If all this makes a god . . . or is it making something **else?** Do you **like** what you see? Absolute power corrupting **absolutely!**
*Kirk's words reach her. She sees Mitchell for what he **really** is and she knows that she is the **only one** who can **stop** him.*
He's right. It's gone **too far!**

Calling on all her powers she raises her arm and points her hand at Mitchell, sending an **energy bolt** directly at him!

And as his body absorbs the force, it emits a **dazzling glow** and for a moment **his powers fail him!**

But only for a moment! When his strength returns, he too raises his hand and sends forth an equally paralyzing beam at his "fellow god."

Her body radiates at the impact and she falls to the ground!

Summoning her remaining energy, she retaliates with an ***even stronger beam . . . .***

THE GOD TUMBLES!
. . . and even his eyes return to normal!
Realizing that her powers too are fading, Elizabeth yells to Kirk . . .
Hurry, Captain. There isn't much time!

Kirk grabs a heavy rock and prepares to throw it at Mitchell, hesitating only for an instant as he bids goodbye to his friend.
Forgive me, Gary.
But Kirk has used up precious seconds with his farewell and now Mitchell's powers are regenerated!
I will forgive you for a moment, James . . . but your moment is fading!

JAMES R. KIRK
. . . into the grave meant for Kirk!
*As Mitchell starts to pull himself out, Kirk finds the seconds he needs. Desperately he scrambles for the **phaser rifle!***
*Knowing that it has **no effect** on Mitchell, Kirk carefully aims it at the huge **stone formation** directly above the grave . . .*

. . . and sends a **searing beam** that melts part of the rock! A giant boulder is torn from the mountain side and falls down on top of the hole, **sealing the grave and its occupant *FOREVER*.**

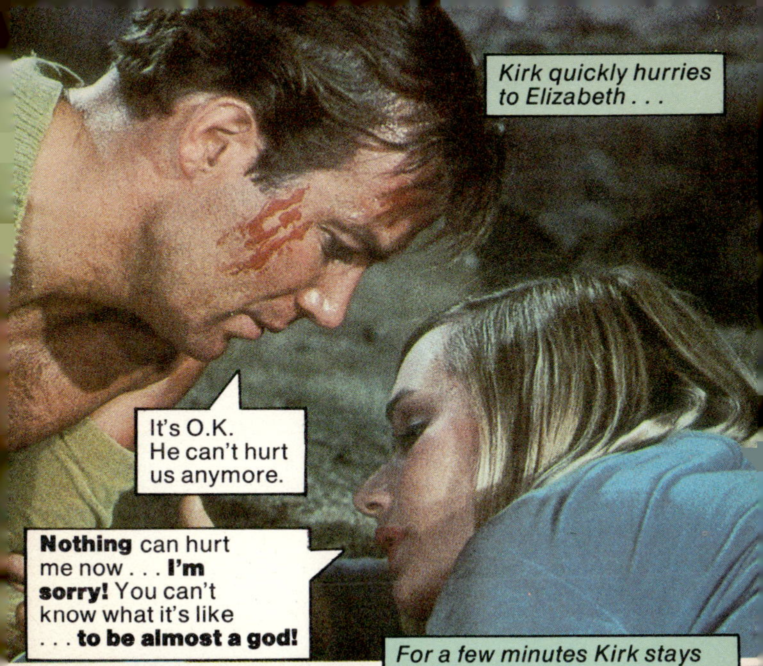

Kirk quickly hurries to Elizabeth . . .
It's O.K. He can't hurt us anymore.
Nothing can hurt me now . . . **I'm sorry!** You can't know what it's like . . . **to be almost a god!**

For a few minutes Kirk stays next to her body, knowing that he can no longer help her but feeling, somehow, that he cannot leave her . . . . not **yet!**

Finally he pulls himself together and reports to the orbiting Starship.
Enterprise from Captain Kirk . . . **Come in . . . .**

Spock here, Captain.
And an exhausted Captain is beamed aboard, back to his grateful crew.

Captain's Log: Stardate 1313.8 — Add to official losses Dr. Elizabeth Dehner. Be it noted that she gave her life in performance of her duty . . . Lt. Gary Mitchell . . . same notation.
I want his service record to end that way. He didn't **ask** for what happened to him.
I felt for him too . . .

Mr. Spock . . . I believe there's **some hope** for you after all!
THE END

GLOSSARY

Bridge — The top deck of a starship from which the Captain, his chief officers and the navigator control the ship.

Communicator — Portable piece of equipment the size of a package of cigarettes used primarily for maintaining communication between landing parties on the surface of a planet and the orbiting spaceship.

Computer Screen — Viewscreen that visually displays information stored in the computer's data banks.

Delta-Vega — An uninhabited fully-automated planet used as a lithium cracking station.

Deflectors — Main defense system utilized by a starship, automatically activated by the ship's computer whenever the vessel encounters hostile matter.

Impulse Power — A starship's back-up method of propulsion, capable of achieving limited speeds.

Lithium — A mineral substance essential in the creation of warp drive power.

Navigator — One who controls the position, course and distance of a starship.

Phaser Rifle — A hand-held weapon with several adjustable settings ranging from "heat activation" to "kill."

Sensor Beam — Scanning equipment capable of sensing and analysing matter in space.

Ship's Log — Record keeping method, used by the Captain, of all activities aboard a starship.

Sickbay — The area of a starship where all major medical procedures are performed.

Transporter — Used to move crew and/or cargo from a starship to planets and back by changing the object's original molecular structure into energy which is beamed to a predetermined point where the original molecular formation is reconstructed.

Turbolift — Elevator-type compartments connecting the 11 decks of a starship, capable of moving horizontally and vertically and operated either manually or by voice.

United Federation of Planets — Democratic alliance of planets comprised of several solar systems, including Sol. All decisions affecting member planets are made through delegates to the Federation Council.

Viewscreen — Electronic devices located throughout the ship that put crew members in visual contact with all other areas of the ship. The major viewscreen is located at the front of the bridge and is capable of displaying, at various magnifications, all matter in the ship's path.

Vulcans — Race inhabiting the planet Vulcan, recognizable by their highly developed intelligence, pointed ears, upswept eyebrows and sallow complexion. Their lives are ruled primarily by logic, not emotion.

Warp Drive — Method of propulsion exceeding the speed of light, using integrated matter and anti-matter.

Yeoman — Clerical/secretarial position on board a starship.

STAR TREK QUIZ #2

In each question below, circle the one answer that best completes the sentence.

1. **One of the first signs that Mitchell has gained ultra-human powers is his:**
   a. commandeering the space shuttle
   b. incredible ability to read
   c. constant concern with food
   d. lack of interest in women
2. **Dr. Elizabeth Dehner has been assigned to the *Enterprise* to:**
   a. replace Dr. Piper
   b. study crew reactions to emergencies
   c. prepare a report on the tribbles' reproductive systems
   d. administer tests on ESP
3. **Kelso is killed:**
   a. by a phaser rifle
   b. when he tries to leave Delta-Vega
   c. by the force field
   d. because Mitchell wills it
4. **The *Valiant* was destroyed by:**
   a. an extra-galactic energy field
   b. the ship's deflectors
   c. its Captain
   d. a faulty sensor beam
5. **Delta-Vega is:**
   a. a lithium cracking station
   b. the home planet of the U.S.S. *Valiant*
   c. an uncharted Earth base
   d. a planet abandoned after a Klingon attack

6. The Transporter is used to:

a. identify and classify matter
b. defend a starship
c. move crew and cargo
d. record the Captain's log

7. The main purpose of the *Enterprise*'s five year mission is to:

a. guard against invasions
b. direct space shuttle activities
c. train new crews
d. explore new worlds

8. The shirts of crew members assigned to the engineering staff are:

a. red
b. green
c. blue
d. orange

9. Spock seldom:

a. talks
b. smiles
c. eats
d. sleeps

10. The planet Terra is also known as:

a. Vulcan
b. Klingon
c. Deneb IV
d. Earth

Turn the page for the answers.

And he pushes the rock out of Kirk's hands with such a sudden force that Kirk is **hurled to the ground!**

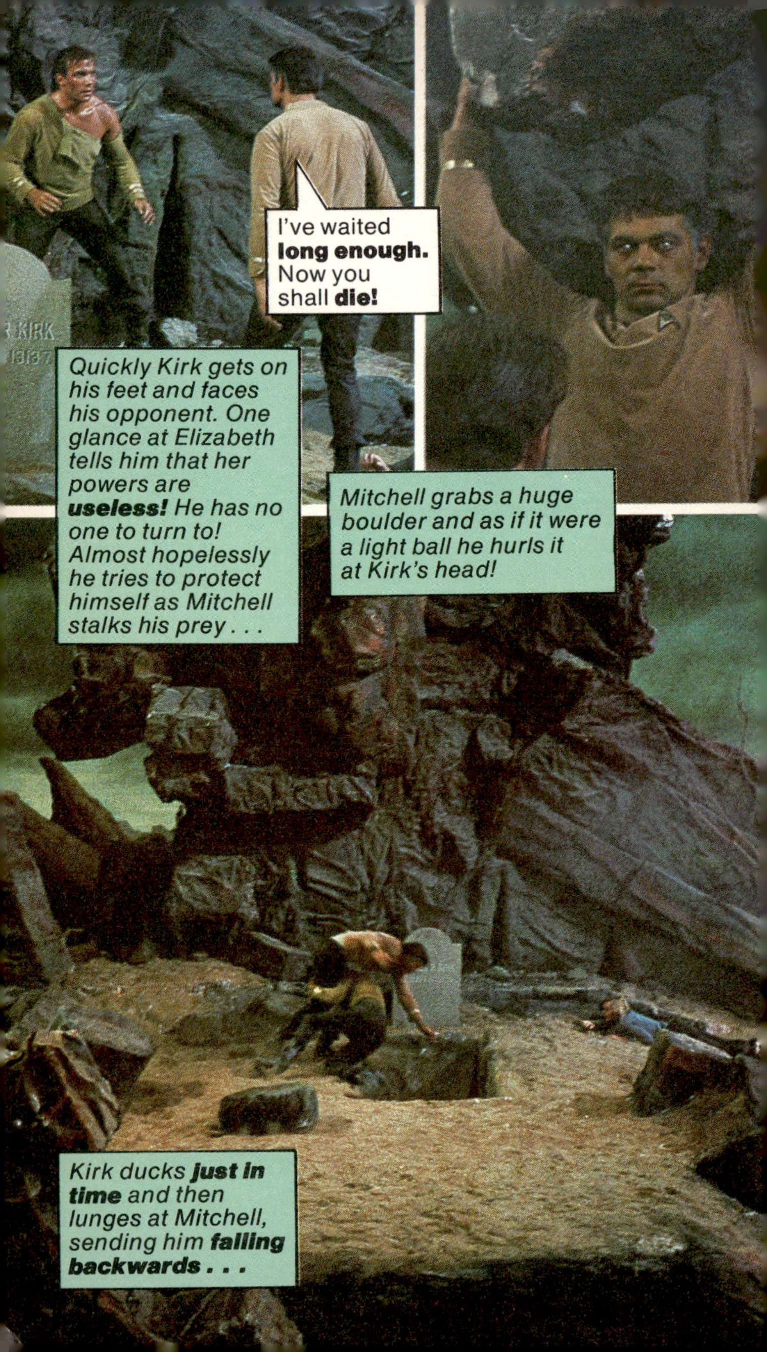
I've waited long enough. Now you shall die!
Quickly Kirk gets on his feet and faces his opponent. One glance at Elizabeth tells him that her powers are useless! He has no one to turn to! Almost hopelessly he tries to protect himself as Mitchell stalks his prey . . .
Mitchell grabs a huge boulder and as if it were a light ball he hurls it at Kirk's head!
Kirk ducks just in time and then lunges at Mitchell, sending him falling backwards . . .

Tribble: a small, furry creature measuring 3" to 7" in length. Extremely affectionate, purrs softly when exposed to most people.

Sounds adorable, right?

And when Lt. Uhura receives one as a gift, **what** could be nicer? Who **wouldn't** love a soft fluffy little pet like a tribble? **No one,** right? **WRONG!!!** Because there is no such thing as **A Tribble.** Tribbles are practically **born pregnant,** bearing litters **every 12 hours!** They seem to be able to reproduce **at will.** And as the crew of the U.S.S. Enterprise soon finds out, they are **exceedingly** willing.

Within days, the Starship is **completely overrun** with darling little tribbles.

And what **might** have stayed merely an inconvenience becomes a **major crisis** when the tribbles eat the **entire supply** of a highly valuable wheat hybrid that Captain Kirk has been ordered to guard from the Klingons. And soon, hundreds of tribbles are found **dead.**

Someone, **somehow**, has **deliberately** poisoned the precious cargo. But who? Captain Kirk and Mr. Spock must move quickly to find that person, before more than just **tribbles** are found dead!

ANSWERS **to Quiz on preceding pages.**

1.**b** 2.**b** 3.**d** 4.**c** 5.**a** 6.**c** 7.**d** 8.**a** 9.**b** 10.**d**